Deep-Sea Tales

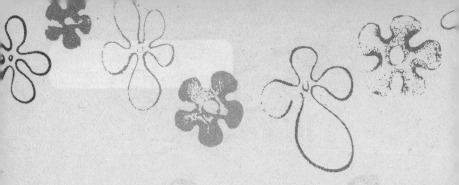

Stephen Hillenburg

Based on the TV series *SpongeBob SquarePants*®
created by Stephen Hillenburg as seen on Nickelodeon®

SIMON SPOTLIGHT
An imprint of Simon & Schuster Children's Publishing Division
1230 Avenue of the Americas, New York, New York 10020

ISBN 0-689-87704-8

These titles were previously published individually by Simon Spotlight.

0211 OFF

Deep-Sea Tales

Simon Spotlight/Nickelodeon

New York   London   Toronto   Sydney

Table of Contents

Tea at the Treedome

by **Terry Collins**

illustrated by **Mark O'Hare**

based on an original teleplay by

**Peter Burns, Mr. Lawrence,
and Paul Tibbitt**

chapter one

Welcome to the sea. Beautiful, mysterious . . . and wet.

It is here where the dolphin frolics and the electric eel slithers. Where the shy octopus plays and the sea horse rides. But go farther down . . . all the way to the bottom of the ocean. Here is a world entirely different from what we know on dry land.

A strange world with different rules, funny customs . . . and unusual creatures.

"Wow! Four stingers!" a squeaky voice exclaimed as an angry jellyfish buzzed by. "Buzz away, jellyfish," the yellow box-shaped character continued in his best dramatic voice. "For soon you shall belong to . . . *SpongeBob SquarePants!*"

SpongeBob gave a few practice swings with his net in preparation to capture his prey.

Then, he readied himself as the jellyfish came around for another pass.

"Buzzzzzzzzzz," said the jellyfish.

SpongeBob buzzed back in his best jellyfish impersonation to lure him into his trap. "Steady," he whispered, readying his net. "Steady . . ."

The jellyfish slowed down and hovered over a blue sea anemone.

"Yes!" SpongeBob screeched, bounding out of hiding and bringing down his net.

The jellyfish avoided the attack and swam to the left.

SpongeBob followed suit, swinging the net in a

sideways arc . . . but somehow caught himself instead!

Hanging in his own net, SpongeBob watched sadly as the jellyfish zipped home to Jellyfish Fields.

Disappointed, SpongeBob continued to look for other jellyfish, but none were to be found. However, he did notice a funny-looking creature in a space suit wrestling a giant clam. . . .

SpongeBob did a double take. Space suit!? Could it be . . . space aliens?

He wiggled out of his net and ran toward the scene.

Upon closer inspection, SpongeBob saw that the space suit was actually a white high-tech diving suit. As for the clam . . . well, it was huge! And mean!

The spry fighter growled like a grizzly bear and used a combination of judo and karate—plus some moves SpongeBob had never even seen

before—to fight the threatening clam.

The creature in a space helmet gave a final cry of triumph and conked the gray shell of the giant clam. It was this move that allowed SpongeBob to clearly see the fighter's face for the first time.

Where have I seen this before? SpongeBob wondered. Reaching into his pocket, he took out his handy *Barks Junior Field Guide*.

SpongeBob frantically flipped through the pages. "Ah-ha!" he cried, finding a page with a picture of the being in the diving suit. However, in the field guide, a furry head was exposed.

"Land squirrel," SpongeBob read aloud. "She's a land squirrel . . . whatever *that* is."

Suddenly, the squirrel gave out a loud grunt of surprise as the clam bit her leg.

"That little squirrel is in trouble!" SpongeBob announced. "This looks like a job for . . . SpongeBob!"

chapter two

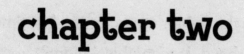

SpongeBob hiked up his square pants and raced to the land squirrel's rescue.

As he ran down the hill, he saw the squirrel jerk her leg free.

Gaining the upper paw, she began battering the clam like a loose penny in a supercharged washing machine!

"Take that! And this! And a mouth of that!" the squirrel cried in a strong Texas accent as she socked and stomped.

The clam rocked back and forth, weakening from the attack.

SpongeBob was fascinated. He'd never seen *anyone* like this squirrel person.

"Y'all need to learn some manners!" the squirrel snorted as she picked up her enemy and held it above her head.

SpongeBob closed his eyes in fear. The clam was ten times bigger than the little land squirrel! If she dropped it, she'd be squished like a bug!

SpongeBob opened his eyes just in time to see the feisty squirrel body slam the battered clam into the sand face first!

"There!" she said. "Mean ol' clam. You know, you're 'bout as ugly as homemade soup!"

"Hooray, land squirrel!" SpongeBob cheered. He was amazed at what he had seen. He *had* to befriend this brave warrior!

Just then, SpongeBob saw the giant clam wiggle like a worm on a hook, trying to pull itself from the silt and muck on the ocean floor.

"Look out!" SpongeBob yelled. But his warning was too late!

The monster clam was free and was heading for the land squirrel!

The clam soared through the air . . . and tumbled toward the unsuspecting squirrel! She never knew what hit her as the clam's maw snapped shut like a bear trap, trapping her inside!

"Hold on, little squirrel!" SpongeBob yelled, his scrawny legs a blur as he raced to his new companion's rescue.

To fight this foe, SpongeBob would need to call on the discipline of . . . karate.

He struck a pose, one skinny arm crooked into the shape of a striking cobra.

"Yah! Ha! Hweee!" he shouted, using the battle cries of a karate master.

"You have fought well, giant clam," said

SpongeBob, honoring his opponent. "Prepare to be vanquished!"

First he hopped onto his oversized enemy. Then, reaching down with both hands, SpongeBob gripped the stiff upper lip of the oversized clam and pulled with all of his might.

SpongeBob gritted his teeth and gave a final Herculean effort—an effort so great, the snap of his square pants popped off!

"HYNUHH!" SpongeBob grunted. "HYNUHH!"

And then, the mouth of the mammoth clam began to inch open with a creaking sound. SpongeBob was so amazed, he nearly let go. "Hey!" he said in disbelief. "I'm actually doing it."

What SpongeBob could not see was the land squirrel pushing the clam's giant jaws open from inside.

"YA!" the squirrel snarled from behind the glass of her helmet as she struggled to free herself. "Yah! Yah! Yah!"

As the clam bucked like an angry bull, SpongeBob was tossed into the air. The squirrel hopped out of the clam's mouth and landed on her feet, ready for more action.

But, before she could make a move, SpongeBob reentered the fray. "Your shell is mine!" he said determinedly as he grabbed the giant's muscular tongue.

The squirrel gaped in surprise, right before the clam's mouth slammed shut, trapping the heroic SpongeBob inside!

chapter three

"Hold on there, little square dude!" the squirrel cried. "I'm a'comin'!"

She flipped the clam up like she was tossing a coin. When it landed, the fighting squirrel then moved on to some of her expert karate moves.

"Yah!" she cried, unleashing a karate chop!

"Hah!" she added, uncoiling a karate kick!

"Yah-hah!" she finished, unspooling a series of master moves, making the clam spin like a top.

The clam's mouth fell open, and a dazed and

confused SpongeBob staggered out.

"Wha' happened?" SpongeBob asked, dizzy from his wild ride inside the mollusk.

The squirrel stomped on the edge of the clam's lip with her boot, and it stood up on one end. She then proceeded to spin the shelled creature like a top, punching and jabbing at a rapid pace before delivering a final uppercut that sent the clam sailing up, up, and far away toward the forbidden lands of Jellyfish Fields!

"Howdy!" the squirrel said, looking down at SpongeBob.

"Hey!" SpongeBob said brightly. "You like karate too!"

The squirrel obliged by assuming the pose of the swooping crane.

"Awesome! So, what's your name?" SpongeBob asked.

"Sandy," she said. "Sandy Cheeks."

Sandy leaped up and went through a series of

karate fighting stances. "What do y'all call yourself?" she asked as she moved across the ocean floor.

SpongeBob grinned and ran toward a curved wall. "I'm . . . SpongeBo-o-o-o-o-o-ob!" he yelled as he ran up the wall, executed a perfect backflip, and landed at a forty-five-degree angle on the corner of his head directly in front of Sandy.

"Well, SpongeBob, take a gander at this!" Sandy announced, leaping over to a rock the size of SpongeBob's pineapple home in Bikini Bottom.

Closing her eyes, Sandy summoned up all of her inner strength and, without a sound, gave the massive boulder a single karate chop.

All was still.

Then, the rock began to vibrate, sending ripples through the water.

The rock continued to shake, finally exploding into a million tiny pieces that scattered in all directions.

A stray pebble bounced off SpongeBob's forehead. "Ooh," he said, dumbfounded at the little squirrel's amazing display of karate.

Snapping out of his trance, SpongeBob tried to act unimpressed. "Oh, yeah?" he said nonchalantly. "Watch this!"

SpongeBob raised his arms, and then, faster than the eye could follow, stuck his right hand into the groove of his left armpit. "Observe," he said.

Then, he pumped his left arm up and down. BRAAAAP! BRAAAAP! BRAAAAP!

Sandy fell back on her tail with an uncontrollable case of the giggles.

After regaining her composure, she gave SpongeBob a playful chop on the top of his square head. "I like you, SpongeBob. We could be tighter than bark on a tree!"

SpongeBob leaped up, copying Sandy's karate move and chopping her on the glass helmet she wore. "I like you, too, Sandy. Hai-YAH!"

BONK!

"Yeow!" SpongeBob cried, his tiny yellow hand aching from the mock blow. "What is that thing on your head, anyway?"

"Why, that's my air helmet," Sandy replied, knocking the thick glass with her knuckles.

"Neat!" SpongeBob said. "May I try it on?"

Sandy laughed. "Heck, no!" she said. "I need it to breathe. I gotta have my air."

Not wanting to be left out of a good thing, SpongeBob announced, "Me too. I love air! Air is good!"

The squirrel looked at SpongeBob in shock. "No kiddin'?" she asked.

SpongeBob flashed Sandy his most confident grin. "No kiddin'!" he said.

Truth be told, SpongeBob wasn't sure what this *"air"* was.

But if his new friend liked it so much, why, he was sure air had to be a most excellent thing!

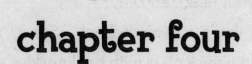

chapter four

"Yup, air's my middle name!" SpongeBob said, sticking his hands in his pockets and rocking on his heels. "The more air the better! Can't get enough of that air!"

Sandy clapped her paws together with delight. "Shee-oot! That's great!"

SpongeBob blushed and smiled. He was starting to love this air stuff!

Sandy reached into a pouch of her diving suit and took out a sheet of paper and a pencil.

Scribbling quickly, she handed SpongeBob a freshly drawn map to her place.

"How about coming over this afternoon to my treedome for tea and cookies, then?" she said. "How does three o'clock sound?"

"Super!" SpongeBob said. He was so excited, his body slowly started to float, allowing his feet to levitate above the ocean floor.

"Well, I gotta mosey on back," Sandy said, turning to go. "Now, don't be late!"

"Okay! See ya later!" SpongeBob said, waving good-bye. He continued to float, watching and waiting until Sandy disappeared.

Then, panic struck!

"Patrick! Patrick! Patrick!" SpongeBob yelled as he raced home. Turning around the corner, he jogged past his own orange pineapple home, past the Tiki-head lair of his neighbor Squidward, and approached a large rock at the other end of the street.

"Patrick!" SpongeBob called. "Patrick!"

Taking a nap on top of the rock was a pudgy pink starfish in blue Hawaiian shorts.

This was Patrick Star, SpongeBob's best friend.

"Patrick, wake up!" SpongeBob called as he bounced with glee. "What's air?"

Patrick lifted up his green sunglasses and peered down at SpongeBob. "Huh?" he said with a yawn. "What's going on?"

SpongeBob stood tall and announced, "Well, I just met this girl, and she invited me to a tea party, and—"

"Way to go, SpongeBob!" the starfish interrupted, giving his buddy a hearty thumbs-up.

SpongeBob returned the thumbs-up. "Thanks. But, get this . . . she wears a hat full of air."

"A hat full of *hair?*" Patrick asked.

"No, air! Air!" SpongeBob corrected.

Patrick's wide smile turned into a look of confusion. He puzzled over SpongeBob's statement for a moment, and finally asked, "Do you mean she puts on airs?"

SpongeBob shrugged his skinny shoulders. "I guess so," he said.

Patrick slid down the rock and stood in front of his pal. "No problem," he said. "Puttin' on airs is just fancy talk. If you wanna be fancy, I can help."

"Really?" SpongeBob said.

"Sure," Patrick replied, holding up one arm and sticking his little finger out. "Now, if you want to impress her, just hold your pinkie like this. The higher you hold it, the fancier you are."

SpongeBob lifted a crooked pinkie. "How's that?" he asked.

"Higher!" Patrick commanded, thrusting his own pinkie into the sky.

SpongeBob followed suit, sticking his pinkie up as far as his spindly arm would stretch. "Like that?" he asked in a pained voice.

Patrick nodded. "Now, that's fancy! They

should call you *SpongeBob FancyPants!*"

SpongeBob took out the map to Sandy's house and held it high above his head, pinkie extended. "Ready, coach!"

Patrick rubbed his chin. "Something's missing," he said. Looking over at Squidward's house, the hefty starfish spotted what he was seeking. "Wait a sec," he said, bounding across his neighbor's front yard.

Squidward popped his head out of his second-story window. "Stay off my lawn, you blob!" he yelled in a whiny voice. "That goes for you, too, SpongeBob!"

"Hi, Squidward!" SpongeBob replied. "I'm going to a tea party!"

"Like I care," Squidward retorted, and slammed his window shut.

Patrick jogged back over and handed a bouquet of bubble-tip sea flowers to SpongeBob. "I borrowed these from Squidward's garden," he

said. "Can't go to a girl's house without flowers!"

SpongeBob slapped his square forehead with his hand. "Duh! I should've known that!"

Patrick winked. "That's what you've got me for!"

As the two buddies left Bikini Bottom and made their way toward Sandy's treedome, Patrick continued to lecture on the finer points of going to a tea party.

"Good manners are important, SpongeBob," the starfish said. "You should say yes and no and thank you and please, and never, *ever*, ask for anything unless your host offers it to you first."

"Yes. No. Thank you. Please. Don't ask. Got it," SpongeBob replied.

Sandy's map was easy to read, and soon enough they were outside her bubble-shaped home.

Patrick took up position outside the protective dome and gave SpongeBob a final pep talk. "Remember," he said. "When in doubt, pinkie out. You can do it, SpongeBob! I'll be watchin'."

chapter five

SpongeBob stepped up to the front door of the treedome. The heavy door was made of thick steel, and it took all of SpongeBob's strength to swing it open.

Once inside, the sponge walked down a narrow hallway and faced a second door identical to the first, only this one was locked. He pressed the button of an intercom, and Sandy's voice came out of the speaker. "Hello?" she said. "Who is it?"

"Hiya, Sandy. It's me. SpongeBob."

"Hold on a sec," Sandy replied from within. "I'll empty the air lock."

Suddenly, a Klaxon horn started to honk!

"Gah!" SpongeBob cried. "What's that?"

He became even more worried when a red light began to flash!

All of a sudden, the water began to go down the drain in the floor. SpongeBob struggled with the door, but it wouldn't open. He began to wheeze. The flowers from Squidward's yard sagged in SpongeBob's hand. His body started to sag as well. SpongeBob felt . . . lightheaded. His eyes bulged in their sockets as he started to cough.

"Sandy! Sandy! Open up!" he screamed. "Open the door, Sandy!"

The land squirrel swung open the steel door to her home. "What's the rush?" she asked.

SpongeBob didn't answer as he fell to the ground on his face, flopping around like a goldfish out of its bowl.

Flipping over onto his back, SpongeBob looked up at Sandy. "Something's gone terribly wrong!" he gasped. "There's no water in here!"

Sandy helped SpongeBob to his feet. "'Course there's no water, silly. Nothin' in here but air!"

Even as he felt his brain beginning to dry out, SpongeBob tried to focus on what Sandy was saying. "No . . . water?" he wheezed.

"Nope! Just good, clean Texas air!" Sandy said. "That ain't a problem, is it?"

SpongeBob gave the squirrel a ghastly grin as his brittle lips peeled back from his teeth. "Problem? Ha-ha! Nope, nothing wrong here!"

"Yee-haw!" Sandy cried, chopping the air as she practiced her karate. "That's what I like to hear! We can work on our moves together!"

SpongeBob, his face still trapped in the awful smile, nodded in agreement. He wasn't sure what Sandy had said, since without any water his ears weren't working properly, but he wasn't about to turn back now.

Without the bulky diving suit, Sandy looked quite different. She had brown fur and was dressed in a pink polka-dot bikini top and skirt.

"Yup, that's how I like my air," SpongeBob said, taking in a deep breath. "Dry as dirt . . . with no water!"

"All right!" Sandy cheered, doing a cartwheel. "I made Texas Tea and El Paso Grande Hot Spicy Cookies! Come on in, I'll give ya the grand tour!"

She skipped across the grass, expecting SpongeBob to follow.

But SpongeBob couldn't move. His legs were like baked clay, and locked in place.

Sandy glanced back over her shoulder. SpongeBob still had the same creepy smile, only more of his teeth were now showing as the skin on his face continued to tighten in the hot sun.

"You sure are a funny little dude," Sandy

snorted as she hopped behind SpongeBob and pushed him toward the picnic table under her giant oak tree.

"Thank you," SpongeBob replied as they sat down at the table. As his knees bent, they made loud popping noises, like firecrackers.

"So, this is my own private little air bubble," Sandy said, chattering away. "This air is the driest, purest, most airiest air in the whole dang sea!"

SpongeBob gasped in agreement.

Sandy pointed to a birdbath made of stone. "Over there is my birdbath."

Inside the birdbath, an orange bird played happily in the water.

Water!

Never had that word sounded so beautiful to SpongeBob.

Sandy babbled on, paying no mind to her guest's distress. "That's my oak tree!" she said, pointing up. "It provides me with extra air!"

SpongeBob nodded once as he focused on the birdbath.

The bird chirped happily, splashing as it bathed, throwing away precious glistening drops of cool, wet water.

"This dome is made of polyurethane. That's a fancy name for plastic," Sandy continued. "Ain't that the bees knees?"

SpongeBob wheezed in agreement, waiting for his chance. He had to get into that birdbath . . . before it was too late!

chapter six

The time for SpongeBob to make his move came when Sandy got up to check on her cookies in the kitchen.

In a blur of speed, he leaped across the grass and sprang into the air, landing on his face in the center of the birdbath!

Each and every inch of SpongeBob's body soaked up the precious water, leaving nothing but one angry chattering bird!

Then, like lightning, SpongeBob flew back to

his position across from the returning Sandy, who never knew he had left!

"Do you like my home?" she asked.

"It's very nice," SpongeBob said, sounding like an old, old man as his throat whined for more water. What he had absorbed from the birdbath had been refreshing, but it was not enough.

SpongeBob needed *more* water.

"Over there's my treadmill," Sandy said, pointing to her exercise equipment. "That's how I stay in tip-top shape."

"Water?" SpongeBob said in a faint wisp of a voice.

"You want something to drink? Glad to oblige! Let's have that tea now!" Sandy said, opening the door in the base of the oak tree. "I'll run down and grab us a pitcher!"

After Sandy left for the tea, SpongeBob heard a knocking sound.

He turned and spotted Patrick outside the

dome. Patrick, who was standing in the blue-green waters of the ocean.

"Flowers!" Patrick yelled, but SpongeBob could barely hear him through the thick polyurethane of Sandy's treedome.

The starfish mimed holding up the bouquet of sea flowers.

SpongeBob looked down. His sea flowers were wilting without water.

Kind of like SpongeBob himself.

"Come and get it!" Sandy announced, bringing up the iced tea.

"I brought you some flowers," SpongeBob gasped.

"For little ol' me? How sweet!" Sandy replied, reaching over to take the gift.

SpongeBob's fingers were locked in place, dried like twigs around the stems of the flower arrangement.

"Umph!" Sandy said, tugging away.

SNAP!

Two of SpongeBob's fingers broke as Sandy retrieved the flowers.

Sandy looked down at the fingers and peered closely at SpongeBob. The little yellow sponge was in sad shape. The water from the birdbath was long gone.

"You okay?" a concerned Sandy asked.

"Yyyyesss, I'm okay," SpongeBob replied, his raspy voice now sounding like an old straw broom sweeping across a wooden kitchen floor.

Sandy wasn't so sure, but she didn't want to embarrass her guest. "You know," she said, trying to change the subject, "you're the first sea critter to ever visit!"

"I can't imagine why," SpongeBob said, coughing.

"Me neither," Sandy said, standing up with the flowers. "I'm gonna put these in a vase."

"Take your time," SpongeBob said.

The instant she was gone, SpongeBob lunged for the treedome exit, but his legs were as stiff as dried leather. He could no longer bend his knees.

I've got to get out of here, SpongeBob thought.

Too hot.

Too dry.

"Must . . . escape . . . treedome," SpongeBob whispered. "Must escape . . . *now!*"

chapter seven

SpongeBob imagined himself turning the knob to the heavy steel door and plunging into wonderful, slippery seawater.

Just then, Sandy reappeared, holding a clear glass vase filled with the sea flowers. "Why, these flowers are just beautiful," the squirrel said as she sat the vase down on the picnic table. "And they'll live *much* longer in a vase of ice . . . cold . . . water."

I don't need it. I don't need it, SpongeBob thought

to himself, repeating the phrase over and over . . . staring at the vase of flowers in front of him.

A vase filled with water and cubes of ice! Ice water!

SpongeBob felt like crying, but he was so dried out, he had no tears left.

"So, tell me about yourself. It must be fascinating being a sea critter!" Sandy said brightly, trying to make conversation.

"Some days are better than others," SpongeBob rasped.

"I can't imagine growing up under the ocean. I grew up in wide-open spaces, where I could run and jump in the sun . . . ," Sandy continued dreamily, letting her voice trail off.

"SpongeBob?" she asked, waving a paw in front of his slack-jawed face.

DING!

A bell went off from inside Sandy's kitchen.

"Oh! There's the cookies!" she announced,

running back to the tree. "Be right back."

"I don't need it! I don't need it!" SpongeBob whispered over and over again. Before him sat the vase. Beads of liquid condensation slid down one side of the glass, pooling at the bottom on the table.

Silence.

"I . . . I . . . I . . . NEEEEEEEED IT!" SpongeBob screamed, blasting off like a rocket into the hot Texas air. He shot straight up into the sky, bounced off the roof of the treedome, and landed in a crouch next to the vase of water.

Wheezing in triumph, he snatched the container and threw away the flowers! Picking up the vase in both hands, he was ready to guzzle!

KNOCK! KNOCK! KNOCK!

SpongeBob ignored the sounds. He knew that Patrick was watching this breach of social etiquette with an expression of sheer horror.

"Noooooooooooooo!" the starfish yelled as he

jumped up and down outside of the dome.

SpongeBob managed to turn his dry, brittle neck and look at his friend.

"No, SpongeBob! No! Stop! Pinkie out! Pinkie!" Patrick cried in a faint voice that was muffled by the thick plastic of the protective dome.

SpongeBob didn't care. He greedily gulped down the soothing ice water!

But the puny vase full of water was not enough to quench his need for water! He was a sponge! Sponges need water, and lots of it! Everybody knew that! Air, phooey! Bring on the liquid refreshment!

SpongeBob ran to the exit . . . only to find the way out blocked by his best friend!

"Where do you think you're going?" Patrick asked.

chapter eight

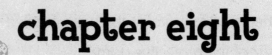

Slamming the steel door shut, Patrick picked SpongeBob up from the grass. "What's wrong, lil' buddy?" he asked.

"I'm a quitter!" SpongeBob sobbed. "Waaaaah!"

Patrick frowned. "You can't leave now, SpongeBob! You'll blow it!" he said.

"Air is not good, Patrick," he said in a defeated tone. "Air is *not* good."

Patrick tucked SpongeBob under one arm like an overdue library book and began the long walk back to the picnic table. "You're just being shy," he said cheerfully. "Don't worry! You're doing fine!

"Nope, not gonna let you blow this," Patrick continued. He gulped. Sandy's picnic table seemed a million miles away. Patrick tried to swallow, but his throat was as dry as a piece of coral.

"Sure is hot in here," the starfish said, dropping SpongeBob and flopping down on the ground. The two friends looked at each other.

"Gosh, SpongeBob," Patrick said, realizing his friend's problem for the very first time. "You don't look so good."

Patrick gasped, but not at SpongeBob's appearance. Suddenly he discovered it was getting very hard to breathe.

His vision was blurring, too. And when he wiped his brow, Patrick discovered his skin felt like it was made of sandpaper! "What kind of place is this?!?" the starfish bellowed.

"T-tr-treedome," SpongeBob answered slowly. "Full of . . . *air.*"

"You mean there's no *water* in here?" Patrick cried, crawling on his hands and knees toward the exit. "We've gotta get outta here!"

"I tried to tell you," SpongeBob said as he crawled after Patrick. "You wouldn't listen."

"I'm listening now!" Patrick yelled. He got to his feet and pounded on the steel door that led out of the treedome. "Let us out! We need water!"

Together Patrick and SpongeBob tried to open the door, but in their weakened condition, they couldn't budge it. Both friends slid to the grass, slumped in defeat.

"Looks like this is the end, old chum," SpongeBob said.

"Next time you get invited to a tea party . . . ," Patrick replied, his voice trailing off.

"Yes?" SpongeBob asked.

Patrick licked his dry lips. "Count me out."

chapter nine

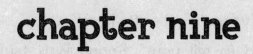

SpongeBob SquarePants was having the most pleasant dream.

He was at a swanky beach party at Goo Lagoon, and all of his friends were there.

Patrick was doing the limbo under a seaweed string, and Mr. Krabs was busy cooking up a grill full of Krabby Patties. SpongeBob's new pal Sandy was lifting weights and impressing everyone with her astonishing strength.

His pet snail, Gary, was off to one side mewing

happily as SpongeBob gave him a pat on the head. Even grumpy old Squidward appeared to be enjoying himself as he played a jazzy tune on his clarinet.

And best of all, there was water everywhere.

He gave a long sigh of relief. Water splashed to his left, and flowed to his right.

SpongeBob opened his eyes. A familiar blue-green haze hung in front of his vision like a curtain.

He smacked his lips. Something tasted wet!

Could it be . . . ? Yes, it was water! Sweet, sweet water!

"Rise and shine, SpongeBob," Sandy said. "Y'all gave me quite the scare! You two were dried up like beef jerky on a North Dallas blacktop!"

SpongeBob looked up and saw Sandy was standing on a ladder. She was holding a garden hose. A steady stream of water was pouring out of the hose and into the open tops of the glass

helmets that SpongeBob and Patrick were now wearing.

"I modified some of my old air helmets," Sandy said. "Turns out they hold water just as good as air!"

SpongeBob stood up and stretched as Sandy finished filling his helmet.

"There, that oughta do it," she said, turning off the hose. "How do you feel?"

"Like a brand-new sponge!" SpongeBob replied.

"Me too!" Patrick added. "Well, maybe not like a sponge, but I feel brand-new."

SpongeBob looked down at the tops of his sensible black shoes. He couldn't look Sandy in the eye. "I'm sorry for all the trouble," he said.

The squirrel laughed. "Weren't no trouble. If ya'll needed water . . . you shoulda asked!"

"Yeah, SpongeBob," Patrick said. "You should have asked."

SpongeBob glared Patrick. "As I recall," he said in a frosty tone, "someone taught me asking for stuff at a tea party was bad manners."

"Really?" Patrick said innocently. "Who was that?"

Stepping off the ladder, Sandy fetched a tray with three glasses of home-brewed Texas Iced Tea and a platter of cookies. "Well, now that you're back to normal, let's have our goodies," she said.

Everyone took a glass of tea.

"I propose a toast," Sandy announced, holding out her glass. "To new friends!"

"To new friends," SpongeBob and Patrick agreed, tilting their glasses for a drink . . . and spilling the tea down the fronts of their water helmets.

"Hold on a second," Sandy said. "I got an idea."

She climbed back up the ladder and dropped a tea bag into SpongeBob's and Patrick's helmets.

Inside the glass containers the water started to change color from pale blue into a lovely golden shade of brown.

"Drink up!" Sandy announced.

"Ahem." Patrick cleared his throat. He then held up his pinkie.

SpongeBob giggled and held up his pinkie too.

Sandy shrugged. She was still getting used to the strange ways of these sea critters. She also stuck out her pinkie.

Everyone took a long, cool drink of their tea and smiled.

"Ahhhhh!" SpongeBob said. "Delicious!"

Naughty Nautical Neighbors

by **Annie Auerbach**

illustrated by **Mark O'Hare**

based on an original teleplay by

Sherm Cohen, Aaron Springer,

and **Mr. Lawrence**

chapter one

Deep in the Pacific Ocean, way below the tropical isle of Bikini Atoll, lies the underwater city of Bikini Bottom. It isn't on any map because no one could possibly chart a place like Bikini Bottom! In this underwater paradise, fish walk, clams talk, and the Krusty Krab— home of the Krabby Patty—is just down the block.

Bikini Bottom is also the home of Squidward Tentacles. Just about everything annoys this whiny and bitter squid. If Squidward had his way, he would be left alone to play his beloved clarinet and work on his gallery of self-portraits.

On one particular day, Squidward was cooking up a simply spectacular dish.

"Woooooow!" Squidward exclaimed, admiring his work. "This is the best soufflé I've ever created!"

The soufflé was in the shape of a little mountain. On top sat a miniature version of Squidward, sitting on a throne under a little palm tree. He looked like the king of the world—or at least the king of *his* little world.

Squidward tasted his culinary creation. "Mmmmm . . . congratulations, Chef! You're a genius!" he declared. "But, wait! A dish like this calls for my best eating attire."

Quickly, Squidward threw off his apron. He

jumped into a bath and started scrubbing.

"I am the greatest chef on the ocean floor," he sang at the top of his lungs. *"There's no one better than me!"*

When he was squeaky clean, Squidward hopped out of the bath, grabbed a towel, and dried around each of his numerous suction cups. Finally, he put on his best pressed suit.

"Well, I look stunning, if I do say so myself," he said. "And I do!" Then, licking his chops, he added, "And now . . . it's time to eat!"

Sitting down at the table, he picked up a knife and fork. Squidward was about to dig in when he heard a familiar sound. A sound that would make his hair stand up—if he had any. A sound that annoyed him twenty-four hours a day . . . the sound of SpongeBob SquarePants!

"Tee-hee-hee!" came from outside Squidward's window.

"Oh, no!" Squidward groaned.

"Tee-hee-hee!" was heard again.

Squidward stood up and went to the window to see his nightmare come true: There sat SpongeBob SquarePants with his best friend, Patrick Star. All three of these nautical neighbors lived next door to each other in this area of Bikini Bottom.

"There goes my peace and quiet!" complained Squidward.

SpongeBob and Patrick were sitting on opposite sides of Squidward's pathway, playing a game. They each had a bottle of bubbles and a bubble wand. One would whisper into a bubble, and the bubble would then float over to the other friend and "pop" out a message. It was their favorite game.

SpongeBob dipped his bubble wand. Then he whispered into it and sent it off toward

Patrick. When the bubble reached him, it popped and said: "Hi, Patrick."

"Tee-hee-hee!" giggled Patrick.

Squidward didn't find this funny at all. To him it was just *extremely* annoying.

Patrick dipped his bubble wand, whispered a message into a new bubble, and sent it SpongeBob's way. When it popped, he heard: "Hey, SpongeBob!"

"Tee-hee-hee!" SpongeBob laughed.

Squidward sighed. "How did I ever get surrounded by such loser neighbors?"

Then it was SpongeBob's turn again. He took a deep breath and exhaled a whisper into a bubble: "Patrick, you're my best friend in the whole neighborhood."

"Aarrgghh!" Squidward couldn't take it anymore. "I must figure out how to shut those two up!" An evil plan quickly formed in his squishy head. He went over to his soufflé and drained some of the liquid out and into a cup. He stirred it vigorously until it began to foam up. Then he, too, blew a message into a bubble and sent it out his window toward Patrick.

Squidward's bubble caught up with another bubble that was already making its way toward Patrick. It was a bubble showdown! But Squidward's evil bubble soon kicked the other bubble into the deep blue sea, never to be heard from again.

The "evil" bubble popped near Patrick's ear. It was Squidward imitating SpongeBob: "Patrick, you are the dumbest idiot it has ever been my misfortune to know."

"What?" said Patrick. He immediately whispered a message into another bubble and sent it to SpongeBob: "Do you really think that, SpongeBob?"

Of course, SpongeBob knew nothing about Squidward's dirty tricks. He didn't know that Squidward was imitating him and calling Patrick an idiot. He didn't know that his message about Patrick being his best friend was being replaced with Squidward's mean one.

So, in his good-natured way, SpongeBob sent a bubble to Patrick that said, "Of course, Patrick! Anyone with eyes could see that!"

Patrick was shocked. "That's it!" he declared, and blew into another bubble. "Well, I think you're ugly! And . . . and . . . yellow is ugly!"

"Patrick, what are you talking about?!" asked a very confused SpongeBob. Then Squidward decided it was time to stir up even more trouble. He immediately made more and more bubbles to send out. Imitating Patrick,

Squidward whispered into a few bubbles and sent them in SpongeBob's direction. The first one popped: "SpongeBob, I no longer wish to know you."

SpongeBob couldn't believe what he was hearing!

Then another bubble popped in front of SpongeBob: "You give bottom dwellers a bad name!"

"WHAT?!" cried SpongeBob.

And another bubble popped: "If I had a dollar for every brain you don't have, I'd have ONE dollar!"

Squidward couldn't help snickering at his own insults. "This is the perfect revenge to get back at those two!"

Then, imitating SpongeBob, Squidward whispered into a bubble and sent it to Patrick: "Hey, Patrick, I heard there was a job opening down at the pet shop—as some NEWSPAPER!"

"Well, you're a big dummy, you DUMMY!" yelled Patrick.

SpongeBob narrowed his eyes. "Yeah? Well, that means that . . . so are you!" he yelled back.

"Uh . . . dummy!" Patrick shouted.

"Sticks and stones make clog my pores, but names will never hurt me!" replied SpongeBob, his hands on his hips.

As SpongeBob and Patrick continued to argue and call each other names, Squidward took a lawn chair outside. He planted himself ringside, with his soufflé and a fork. "There's nothing better than dinner theater!" He laughed.

"And you're a turkey!" continued Patrick.

"Well, you're a bigger one!" SpongeBob shot back.

Patrick had to think fast. "Well, you're *still* yellow and you know what else is yellow?"

"What?" said SpongeBob.

"YOU ARE!" replied Patrick.

"Oh, good one!" Squidward said with a nod.

SpongeBob couldn't take it anymore. He yelled at Patrick, "Yeah? Well, it doesn't matter what you call me, because I never want to see you again, anyway!"

"I don't want to see you, either!" Patrick replied, and stormed off to his house.

SpongeBob rushed into his own house. "Aw, tartar sauce!" he said, slamming the door.

chapter two

"Ha-ha-ha-ha-ha!" cackled Squidward.

Squidward was laughing so hard, he didn't realize there was still a forkful of food in his mouth. "Ha-ha-ha-ha-ha . . . gulp . . . ccckkkk!" Suddenly he began to choke! Not only was he choking on his soufflé, but on the fork, too!

He tried to swallow. "Gguauu—"

Patrick peeked out from his house and ran outside. "Wow, Squidward, you're choking!" Patrick pointed out.

Squidward just glared at him.

"I know what to do, but I should wash my hands first," Patrick said.

But by this time, Squidward was looking worse. He was turning an even uglier shade of greenish gray.

"Oh, well!" Patrick said, and took a deep breath. He put his mouth over Squidward's and exhaled. The more air Patrick blew into Squidward's mouth, the more Squidward's body began to inflate. Patrick hoped all the air would dislodge the fork. But instead, Squidward's body blew up like a balloon—even the suction cups on all of his arms popped!

Finally, Squidward let out a big breath, and the fork came flying out! It landed right in Patrick's hands.

"Oooh! It worked!" Patrick said, quite pleased with himself.

Thankful to be alive, Squidward gushed, "Wow! Patrick you *saved* me!"

"I did?!" Patrick said.

"Yep!" Squidward declared. "You're a real lifesaver, friend!"

"Friend?" Patrick repeated. "Ooh . . . friend."

Squidward nodded. "Yeah, Patrick," he said casually. "We're friends."

But "friend" was a magic word to Patrick. Now that SpongeBob was out of the picture, Patrick had plenty of time to spend with his *new* friend. "So, what are we doing tonight, best friend?" he asked Squidward enthusiastically.

"Well, I was going to practice my clarinet SOLO," answered Squidward.

"Great! Let's go!" Patrick said, putting an arm around Squidward.

Uh-oh. What have I done? Squidward thought as they went inside.

chapter three

Being next-door neighbors, SpongeBob had easily overheard Patrick and Squidward's conversation. He heard that Patrick *already* had a new best friend.

"Aw . . . who needs 'em!" SpongeBob said firmly. He looked around his home. It was a fully furnished, two-bedroom pineapple. "They're no fun, anyway, right, Gary? Gary?"

Gary, SpongeBob's pet snail, seemed to be busy deep inside his shell at the moment.

"What am I worried about?" SpongeBob said to himself. "I've got plenty of other friends." He looked around and then picked up a pen and drew faces on three of his fingers. "I could name three right off the bat!"

SpongeBob wiggled his fingers. He sighed and said weakly, "Woo-hoo! The gang's all here." Then he began to sob. "I have no friends at all! Patrick's a deserter, and even Gary's too busy for me!"

Suddenly SpongeBob heard Squidward next door. He jumped up and ran to the window to see what was going on.

"Tonight I will be performing my version of Solitude in E Minor," Squidward said.

"E Minor. All right!" cheered Patrick. "Yeah, yeah!"

Squidward just ignored Patrick. Then he took a deep breath and played only one note before he heard, "ZZZZZZZZzzzzzzz."

Patrick had fallen asleep.

"Oh, puh-leeze!" Squidward groaned. "Patrick, wake up! Wake up, you lazy invertebrate!"

SpongeBob giggled as he watched from his window. He knew Patrick wouldn't wake up for anything!

"That's it!" cried Squidward. "I can't play with that annoying racket!" Then he put down his clarinet and went over to the snoring starfish. Yelling at him didn't work. Shaking him didn't work. Even tickling him didn't work. "Oh, why me?" moaned Squidward. "Why me?!"

Finally, Squidward put his arms under Patrick's arms and began to drag him out the front door. "Grr-grunt-grunt!" Squidward groaned.

When he eventually got Patrick outside, Squidward suddenly screeched, "OH! My back! I threw out my back!"

"Oh, boy!" exclaimed SpongeBob, who was still watching from his window. "Now's my chance!"

SpongeBob raced outside. He took a running start and then bounced off his diving board. SpongeBob sailed through the water. Before Squidward knew it, SpongeBob was zooming right at him!

Squidward looked up in horror. "SpongeBob—no!" he shrieked. "Stay back!"

"Hang on!" SpongeBob called, his speed increasing.

"Stay away from me!" Squidward warned.

But SpongeBob was a sponge with a mission. "I'll save you!" he yelled, closing in.

"NO!" Squidward cried. He desperately

tried to get back inside his house. But since he had thrown out his back, he couldn't run away from SpongeBob. He couldn't run at all. In fact, he could barely walk.

Just as Squidward made it back to his front door, SpongeBob plowed right into his back.

"AAARRGGGHHH!" Squidward yelled in pain. "I'm ruined!" Then he moved around a bit and was surprised to find that he actually felt better! "Hey, I feel great! Thanks, SpongeBob, you're a real friend."

SpongeBob's eyes glazed over, and his smile grew. "Fr-iend?" he repeated.

Realizing his mistake, Squidward quickly said, "Uh . . . no! I didn't mean—"

"Don't worry about it, Squiddy, ol' pal!" said SpongeBob. "That's what friends are for."

"Oh, great, *another* friend," said Squidward. "Here we go again. . . ."

chapter four

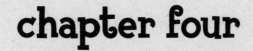

As Squidward went inside his house, he found that SpongeBob was *right* behind him.

"So, dumb Patrick fell asleep on you, huh?" SpongeBob asked.

"Uh-huh," replied Squidward.

"Some friend he is!" said SpongeBob. "A real friend would perform for *you!*"

Suddenly, Squidward perked up. "Do you play?" he asked excitedly.

"Are you kidding?" SpongeBob said,

quickly looking around. "I've been playing the bassinet for years!" SpongeBob lied, grabbing the bass nearby. "Give me an A, buddy!"

Squidward played an A on his clarinet.

SpongeBob took the bow and *tried* to play. The noise he was making was painful. To make matters worse, he began to sing off-key: *"Squidward is my best friend in the world! Squidward is my best friend in the sea!"*

The combination of horrific sounds made Squidward drop his clarinet. "AHHH!" he shouted, cringing.

But SpongeBob kept playing and singing: *"I'm Squidward's very best friend. He doesn't like anyone more than me!"*

SpongeBob was playing the bass with so much gusto that the bow actually got caught and pulled back like an archer's arrow. The bow went flying—and straight into Squidward—a

painting of Squidward, that is. Squidward loved to re-create himself—be it as paintings, wax models, or on the tops of soufflés.

Squidward went over to the painting, angrily pulled out the bow, and broke it in two. "SpongeBob!" he yelled.

SpongeBob just continued. He began to strum the bass like a guitar, instead, singing, *"Squidward—"*

". . . likes Patrick more than SpongeBob!" Patrick chimed in.

SpongeBob whirled around to see Patrick sticking his head through the window. SpongeBob stomped over to it and slammed the window shut. Then he picked up the bass and slammed it on the ground with every word: *"And Patrick is a dirty, stinky, rotten friend stealer!"*

The bass was now in pieces. "Um . . . I can fix this," SpongeBob said, embarrassed.

Squidward's face turned red with anger. His squid blood was beginning to boil!

"Squidward?" SpongeBob said nervously. "Squiddy? Pal? Friend? Buddy? Amigo?"

With one swift kick from Squidward, SpongeBob found himself outside. He picked himself up and uneasily yelled to Squidward, "So, uh . . . I'll see you later? Uh . . . call me!"

chapter five

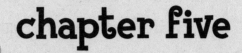

"ICK!" cried Squidward. "That was disgusting. I feel like I need to scrub myself. Maybe I can wash away all that gross 'friendship' talk." He sighed and headed into the bathroom.

"AAAHH!" Squidward shouted suddenly.

Patrick was back—and in the tub! "Hey, *buddy,* I warmed it up for you!" Patrick said. He was holding a bar of soap and a scrub brush.

Squidward had had it! "Patrick, get out!" he

demanded. "And put some clothes on!"

Just then SpongeBob poked his head in through the bathroom window. "I thought I heard some . . . aha! So *this* is what I find, huh? My best friend and my *ex*-best friend! And . . . and . . . rubber bath toys!"

"Oh, yeah? Well, he was my friend first!" Patrick stated.

SpongeBob wasn't about to back down. "Patrick, you're just a backbiting, bathtub-filling, blob of—"

Patrick cut him off. "I'm rubber, you're glue, whatever you say bounces off me and sticks to you!"

"Oh, that's really original," SpongeBob said in a snotty voice. "Besides, you're such a big blob that *everything* bounces off you!"

Squidward looked at the two of them arguing back and forth. He turned and ran out of the bathroom and the house, screaming, "This can't be happening to me!" He hid in a garbage can outside.

Back inside, SpongeBob and Patrick stopped their name-calling long enough to realize that Squidward was no longer there.

"Squidward?" called SpongeBob.

"Hey, Squidward!" Patrick said. "Buddy?"

But there was no way Squidward was going back in the house with his two new "friends."

This is nuts! Squidward thought to himself, still inside the garbage can. Those two are making my life miserable! I need a plan to get them back together and out of my way!

chapter six

The next day, SpongeBob was reading *A Tale of Two Squiddies* when the doorbell rang. An envelope was slipped under his front door.

"What's this?" SpongeBob wondered aloud as he picked it up and smelled it. "Aaaahh . . . Squidward." He tore open the envelope. "A dinner party? Tonight? Thrown by Squidward? I'd love to!" he exclaimed.

Later that day, after a long bath, SpongeBob ran into his bedroom and opened up the closet.

"What to wear, what to wear . . . ," he pondered.

Finally, after careful consideration, SpongeBob chose a white shirt, a red tie, a pair of brown, square pants, and a pair of black shoes. "Perfect," he said as he looked in the mirror. "I'm ready!"

"Squidward!" called SpongeBob as he knocked on his next-door neighbor's door. "Oh, Squidward-iard!"

Inside, Squidward groaned. "Let's get this over with," he said to himself, and opened the door.

"Did you miss me?" SpongeBob asked with a grin.

"Come on in!" Squidward replied cheerfully. "You look stunning!"

SpongeBob beamed. "Gee, thanks! I'd

much rather dine with *you* than that lousy . . . EEK!"

SpongeBob looked across the room to see his ex-best friend, Patrick, sitting at the table!

"Say, what gives? I'm not sitting near that maniac!" insisted SpongeBob.

"Me either!" Patrick added. "This was a setup!"

"But I thought you two were my best friends," Squidward said innocently.

"I *am* your best friend!" SpongeBob quickly said.

"No, *I* am!" Patrick declared.

"I am!" countered SpongeBob.

"Enough!" Squidward screamed. Then, remembering his master plan, he sweetly said, "How about some appetizers, guys?"

Patrick's stomach growled.

"I'll take that as a 'yes,'" said Squidward.

"Be right back," he added, and headed into the kitchen to begin Plan A. . . .

SpongeBob reluctantly took a seat at the table. Immediately, he and Patrick had their backs to each other. Neither one was going to be the first to talk. It was silent for a few minutes, with the only noise coming from Patrick's stomach. The tension in the room was worse than a sea of hungry anchovies.

Luckily, Squidward came back from the kitchen. "Who wants some delicious Krabby Patties?" he asked, holding a plateful of mini burgers.

"Oh! Me! Me!" SpongeBob and Patrick shouted at once. They each greedily grabbed a Krabby Patty off the plate.

"Now, now," Squidward began, "remember your manners. We're all friends here, right?"

SpongeBob put down the Krabby Patty he

was holding. "I'm not friends with *him,*" he said, pointing to Patrick.

Patrick grabbed SpongeBob's Krabby Patty and swallowed it whole. "And I'm not friends with you, either," Patrick told SpongeBob.

"Then how come you ate my Krabby Patty?" asked SpongeBob.

"I was hungry," Patrick explained.

Suddenly it was a mad dash for the Krabby Patties. SpongeBob grabbed a bunch of Krabby Patties in his arms while Patrick grabbed a bunch in his mouth.

Squidward looked at the now empty plate he was holding. He didn't even get to eat one Krabby Patty. He trudged back into the kitchen. "All right, Plan A didn't work, so I guess it's time for Plan B."

chapter seven

Squidward returned to the table with an old-fashioned soda bottle. "How about some soda?" he asked.

"Oh, yes, please!" answered SpongeBob. He held out a cup. "Thanks, *friend! Sluuurrp!*"

"How about some for your best friend?" Patrick asked Squidward, and held out his cup.

But SpongeBob was sneaky and put his own cup under the nozzle first. "Thanks, best friend! *Glug, glug, glug!*"

Patrick looked at Squidward and pleaded, "Can I have some now, buddy?"

"Wait! I need some more!" SpongeBob demanded.

"I still didn't get any!" Patrick said angrily.

SpongeBob took the few drops he had left in his cup and poured it into Patrick's. "There you go!" he said. Then he looked at Squidward and added, "More, please!"

Glug, glug, glug.

"More, Squidward!" said Patrick.

Glug, glug, glug.

"More, Squidward!" said SpongeBob.

Glug, glug, glug.

"More, Squidward!" called Patrick.

Glug, glug, glug.

"More, Squidward!" called SpongeBob.

Glug, glug, glug.

"Squidward!"

"Squidward!"

SpongeBob and Patrick went through one cup of soda after another. Squidward could hardly keep up with them. It seemed that every time he filled one's cup, the other one's was empty.

"Sorry, boys, I'm all out of soda," Squidward finally said. "I'm going to get some more. Why don't you two just stay here and chat?" he said with a sneaky smile, and quickly left.

By this time, SpongeBob and Patrick were so full of soda that they looked like two huge balloons.

"Hiccup!" said SpongeBob.

Patrick tried his hardest not to laugh out loud.

"Hiccup!" repeated SpongeBob.

"Burp!" went Patrick.

SpongeBob couldn't help but giggle.

Patrick couldn't keep it in, either!

All this burping and hiccuping started to make them laugh. And once they started laughing, there was no stopping them. Soon bubbles filled the whole room, and they both started to lift up into the air. They became lighter as they burped out all the gas from the soda.

SpongeBob and Patrick were having so much fun, they forgot why they had even started arguing in the first place.

As the two friends floated in the air, the bubbles kept multiplying. They filled the entire house. Soon the house became too full of bubbles. The house began to shake. It was ready to burst!

Just then, Squidward returned home with more soda. He was about to put his key in the door when—*KABOOM!* Squidward's house exploded!

I should just walk away right now, Squidward told himself. He took a deep breath and fearfully opened the door. Once the bubbles cleared, Squidward looked around at what once was his house. Now it was mostly rubble; no walls were left, not to mention any of the furniture or paintings. The only thing left intact was the door.

Squidward sighed. "What a surprise. I invited them in, and I left them alone. Well, Squidward, what have we learned, today?" He glared at SpongeBob and Patrick, who were standing there, looking innocent.

"Guess what, Squidward?" SpongeBob said excitedly.

"Oh, this should be good . . . ," mumbled Squidward.

Patrick piped up. "Me and SpongeBob are friends again!"

"Great. Go be friends somewhere else," replied Squidward through his teeth.

"Don't you want us to help you clean this up a little?" asked SpongeBob.

"NO! OUT!" Squidward shouted.

SpongeBob and Patrick quickly made their way out past Squidward.

"Psst!" SpongeBob whispered to Patrick. "I think he's jealous."

"How pathetic," Patrick whispered. "Come on. Let's get our bottles of bubbles!"

Squidward slammed the door once they left. A leftover bubble floated by and popped when it hit the door.

BAM!

The door fell over—and right on top of Squidward. "Oh! My back!" he cried. "I'll get you, SpongeBob—once I can move!"

Once again, SpongeBob SquarePants had ruined everything of Squidward's—his back, his house, and especially his day!

Hall Monitor

by **Annie Auerbach**

based on an original teleplay by
Chuck Klein, Jay Lender,
and **Mr. Lawrence**

illustrated by **Mark O'Hare**

chapter one

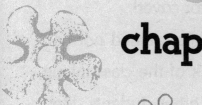

There's no one in Bikini Bottom quite like SpongeBob SquarePants. When he's not at work flipping Krabby Patties or on an adventure with his best friend, Patrick, SpongeBob can be found at Mrs. Puff's Boating School. Mrs. Puff's Boating School is where students learn the rules of the road.

SpongeBob has taken Mrs. Puff's class forty-seven times. He knows the answer to every question *in* the classroom. But when it's time for the driving portion of the exam, SpongeBob always panics behind the wheel and ends up failing. When SpongeBob is on the road, it's best to steer clear—or run for cover!

One day at school, things seemed normal: SpongeBob sat in the back of the class taking precise notes while all the other students slept. Their snoring was almost louder than Mrs. Puff's lecture.

"Everyone wake up!" Mrs. Puff called. "It's time to pick this week's hall monitor."

SpongeBob's sat upright in his seat. He moved his desk out into the center aisle to make sure Mrs. Puff could see him. Being chosen as hall monitor was an honor SpongeBob wanted more than anything. With his eyes wide and hopeful, he wished hard for his name to be called.

Mrs. Puff looked down at the list attached to

her clipboard and said, "Let's see here . . . this week's hall monitor will be . . . um . . . Bart. No, he's done it already. Tina? No, no," she said to herself. Then Mrs. Puff gasped in horror. At the bottom of the list was the name she feared the most: SpongeBob SquarePants!

"It's Jimmy! Jimmy's the hall monitor!" Mrs. Puff exclaimed.

Jimmy, a green fish wearing shorts and a T-shirt, shook his head and said, "Mrs. Puff, I've done it already."

"Oh!" Mrs. Puff replied, quickly scanning the list again. "Bill?"

"No way, Mrs. Puff!" answered Bill, a plump gray fish sitting in the back.

Mrs. Puff wasted no time. "Tina, you're the hall monitor," she said.

"Hey! I've done it three times already," Tina declared, her fins on her hips.

"Uh . . . B-Beth!" Mrs. Puff said. "Yes, Beth!"

"She graduated," Jimmy told her.

By this time, SpongeBob had eagerly inched his desk up the aisle. He could hardly contain his excitement. He knew what was coming.

But Mrs. Puff was still trying to avoid calling the name of a certain rectangular student. "Henry? Vera? Sheldon?" she called out in desperation.

But it was no use.

Mrs. Puff sighed deeply. "All right, I guess I have no choice." She gulped. "The hall monitor of the week is . . . SpongeBob."

"Ya-HOOOO!" yelled SpongeBob.

And so the victory dance began. SpongeBob raced around the classroom, bouncing off the walls and zigzagging around the desks. All the while he shouted, "Hall monitor! Hall monitor! I'm the hall monitor!"

Finally SpongeBob calmed down, stood next to Mrs. Puff in the front of the class, and saluted. "Hall Monitor SpongeBob reporting for duty, ma'am," he said in a drill sergeant voice.

Mrs. Puff began, "Now Sp—"

But SpongeBob continued. "I'm ready to assume my position . . . IN THE HALL!"

"Yes, but—," Mrs. Puff said.

"I will protect all who are weak . . . IN THE HALL!" SpongeBob shouted. "All rules will be enforced IN THE HALL!"

"Okay!" said an annoyed Mrs. Puff. "Just take the cap and belt."

"I can't accept that yet, ma'am," SpongeBob told her. "First I have to make my speech."

Mrs. Puff sighed. "You can't make this easy, can you?"

"CLASSMATES!" SpongeBob began. "Who am I to deserve such a great honor? Why, I'd be nothing without Mrs. Puff."

"Oh, give me a break," Mrs. Puff muttered under her breath.

". . . and to my public," SpongeBob continued, "all I can say is . . . well, frankly, I'm touched." He wiped a tear away. "I want you to know that I represent *you* out there . . . out there IN THE HALL. I will carry out my duties . . . ," SpongeBob promised as he rambled on. ". . . crime and punishment . . . punishment and crime . . . IN THE HALL."

The other students sighed and groaned.

But SpongeBob wasn't done. "That reminds me of an extremely long speech written by the greatest hall monitor of all time." He took a dramatic pause. "Friends, students, juvenile delinquents . . . lend me your ears . . ."

The students covered their ears.

Three hours later, SpongeBob was getting ready to wrap up his speech. Finally he said, "In conclusion, and without a moment to spare, I will put on this uniform and assume my duties as . . . hall monitor!"

SpongeBob had expected a round of applause. But by this time everyone had fallen asleep—including Mrs. Puff. Luckily, the bell rang.

"Zzzzzzz . . . huh? Oh!" Mrs. Puff said as she stood up.

All the students woke up with a jolt and rushed out of the classroom. They practically ran right over SpongeBob on their way out.

"SpongeBob, are you okay?" Mrs. Puff asked.

SpongeBob sighed. "I overdid the speech again, didn't I?" he asked his teacher.

"I'm afraid so," Mrs. Puff told him.

"Aw, tartar sauce!" exclaimed SpongeBob. "I guess I won't be needing these." He handed the hall monitor cap and belt back to his teacher. "I hardly knew ya," he added, looking sadly at the uniform.

SpongeBob was gripping the uniform so tightly that Mrs. Puff had to pry it from his hands. SpongeBob's disappointment showed in his face, as well as in his slightly deflated head.

Mrs. Puff couldn't believe it, but she actually felt sorry for SpongeBob. Each time he'd been elected hall monitor, he hadn't made it out the door. "Uh . . . SpongeBob?"

"Yes, Mrs. Puff?" replied SpongeBob.

"I can at least let you *wear* the uniform until tomorrow," she offered.

"Woo-hoo!" yelled SpongeBob. His head was instantly back to its full size. "Thanks, Mrs. Puff!"

SpongeBob sang to himself as he put on his hall monitor uniform. "Be bop de diddit de doo . . . hall be bop be diddle monitor . . . root toot toot."

Mrs. Puff sighed and shook her head as SpongeBob bounded out the classroom door.

chapter two

Walking proudly in his hall monitor uniform, SpongeBob strode down the street. He held his head up high, honored to be hall monitor, even if it was only for the rest of the day.

Suddenly he stopped dead in his tracks. "A broken traffic light!" he cried. "Hmmm . . . who's to say my monitoring duties should end just because the bell rang?" he wondered. Then he straightened his cap. "I can be helpful anywhere! Yes, this looks like a job for the hall monitor!"

SpongeBob pulled out a whistle. "All right," he said as he signaled. "Hey, big boat, you go that way, and this turbo boat can go this way, and this one that way, and this one left . . . and this one right . . . and over here . . . and over there . . ."

SpongeBob not only made signals with his arms, but with his legs and rear end as well! His arms went left, the cars went right. His legs kicked out, the cars swerved around! No driver could follow. They weren't sure if he was dancing or directing traffic.

"Ha! This is a piece of Krusty Krabcake!" SpongeBob said confidently.

Just then, two boats swiped each side of SpongeBob, sending him spinning. "*Whoa!*" he yelled.

Gaining his balance, SpongeBob looked up to see a huge boat coming right toward him!

With all his might, SpongeBob stretched his legs as far as they would go, just in the nick of time.

"Yikes!" SpongeBob yelled and the big boat zoomed right between his legs.

"Barnacle brain!" yelled the driver.

SpongeBob couldn't really hear him over the traffic noise. "You're welcome!" he called with a friendly wave.

SCREECH!

SLAM!

CRASH!

That "friendly" wave caused the biggest frenzy yet—a fifteen-car pileup! Pedestrians nearly became speed bumps, horns were blaring, and tempers were flaring.

"Well, my work here is done," he said. Then he smiled. "What would this town do without me?"

SpongeBob was so pleased with his first hall monitor task, he had no idea that he had *caused* more accidents than he had prevented! He didn't notice all of the angry drivers, wrecked cars, and injured pedestrians around him.

"On patrol, I'm on patrol," he sang to himself as he left the traffic catastrophe.

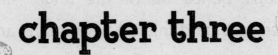

chapter three

SpongeBob was walking home when he heard a noise. "Who's there?" SpongeBob said and froze. He looked at the looming shadow on the wall. "It's a bird . . . it's a plane . . . it's . . . it's . . . Hall Monitor!" he finished with a laugh.

SpongeBob walked a few more feet before another bold opportunity presented itself: a low, open window. "Uh-oh," he said and took a peek.

Inside the house, a couple of fish were enjoying a meal together.

"More seaweed medley, dear?" the female fish asked her husband.

"Oh, yes!" the husband replied. "You know it's my favorite!"

SpongeBob was appalled. "The fools! This open window is so unsafe! They've left themselves susceptible to danger."

Of course, SpongeBob couldn't just *warn* them of this danger. "I must show them the error of their ways . . . *by example!*" he declared.

SpongeBob looked around and grabbed a paper bag out of a nearby garbage can. He put it over his head, punching two holes out for eyes. Then he leaped in the window and screamed, "Oooooohhhh! I'm the Open-Window Maniac!"

"AHHHH!" screamed the husband and wife and ran for their lives.

"I hope you learned a valuable lesson!" SpongeBob called after them. He took a deep breath. "Boy, this hero stuff is hard work! But *someone* has to do it."

SpongeBob continued patrolling the streets of Bikini Bottom. He was so pleased with himself that he started to imagine his future. "With all I've done already, they should make me the permanent hall monitor. I can see it now . . . my picture in the Hall of Hall Monitors. Wanna-be hall monitors will hear stories of my brave monitoring experiences and I'll get the first-ever Hall Monitor medal. I'll give a speech at the Society of Hall Monitors. . . ."

Just then, something caught on SpongeBob's foot, causing him to fly through the air. "*WHOA!*" he yelled.

Once SpongeBob got to his feet, he shouted, "Vandals! Another crime!"

Before him on the ground was a blob of something pink. SpongeBob bent over and scooped up a dollop with his finger. "Mmmm . . . strawberry ice cream," he said, smelling it. "I must *act*! It's my duty as hall monitor to protect and serve. I must find out who's behind this delicious dessert . . . I mean, uh, crime!" He was looking around for any suspects when a dollop of the same strawberry ice cream fell on top of his head.

"Patrick!" exclaimed SpongeBob as he looked up and saw his best friend sitting on a wall.

Patrick looked around and didn't see anyone. He continued licking his ice cream.

"Patrick!" SpongeBob shouted again.

Patrick's eyes widened in fear. "My ice cream! It's alive!" he cried. "Aaaaaahhhhhh!!!" He threw the ice cream up in the air. It went high

in the sky, turned upside down, and started its descent—landing right in SpongeBob's face!

"Down here, Patrick," called SpongeBob, wiping his face.

Patrick looked down and smiled. "Oh, SpongeBob, it's you!"

"Come down here," SpongeBob ordered.

Getting off the wall wasn't too easy for Patrick. He lost his balance and landed right on top of SpongeBob, flattening him like a pancake.

"SpongeBob? SpongeBob, where are you?" Patrick called out.

In a muffled voice, SpongeBob said, "I'm down here!"

Patrick stood up and stared at SpongeBob. "You look funny, SpongeBob!" he said with a giggle.

"That's *Hall Monitor* to you," SpongeBob

corrected as he stood up and expanded back to his normal size.

"Oops. Sorry, Officer," replied Patrick.

"Sorry is not good enough, Patrick," SpongeBob told him. "You've just committed a crime and I'm taking you in!"

"What crime?" Patrick asked nervously.

"Littering!" SpongeBob declared. "Ice cream is meant to go in your mouth—not on the street."

Patrick burst into tears. "Oh, I'm a bad person!" he sobbed. "Boo hoo! Boo hoo!"

Just then a fish selling newspapers approached the pair. "Extra! Extra! Maniac strikes Bikini Bottom! City paralyzed with fear!" he cried and handed them a newspaper. "Take it, friends. Arm yourselves with knowledge!"

SpongeBob began to read. "Hmmm . . .

maniac . . . Bikini Bottom . . . car wrecks . . . a break-in . . ." Then he took a breath and said in his most heroic voice, "Who better to bring this maniac to justice than me . . . Hall Monitor!"

chapter four

SpongeBob turned to Patrick, who was still upset about the ice cream incident. "I can't handle this maniac case alone," SpongeBob explained. "Patrick! Are you ready to give up your life of crime?"

"I want to be GOOD!" cried Patrick.

"Uh-huh. I thought so!" SpongeBob said, proud of his best buddy. "Now you just need a symbol of authority," he added, looking around.

Patrick picked up the ice-cream cone from the ground and put in on his head. It fit perfectly!

"Excellent!" said SpongeBob. "It is our duty to catch this maniac and bring him to justice. But how to proceed?" He looked over at Patrick. "Hey, Deputy, you're an excriminal, what would you do?"

"Hmmm," Patrick thought carefully. "I know! I'd get an ice cream!"

"Let's go!" said SpongeBob.

A little while later, SpongeBob and Patrick emerged from the ice-cream parlor. They each had an ice-cream cone and seventy-five little taster spoons.

Soon they both had licked their ice creams until they were all gone.

"Okay, now what?" asked SpongeBob.

"Seconds?" suggested Patrick.

"I'm ready!" said SpongeBob and they headed back inside.

"Thirds?" Patrick suggested a few minutes later.

"Sure!" replied SpongeBob.

Seven ice creams later, SpongeBob finally said, "Patrick, this isn't working. We're not getting any closer to catching the maniac."

"Yeah," agreed Patrick. "But this ice cream sure is tasty!"

"We've got to do something else," SpongeBob declared. "Something with . . . walkie-talkies!"

"Yaaayy!" cheered Patrick.

SpongeBob pulled out two walkie-talkies, handing one to Patrick. "I think we'll have a better chance of catching the maniac if we split up."

"Awww," Patrick said, disappointed.

SpongeBob put a hand on Patrick's shoulder. In his best hall monitor voice he said, "Remember, it's for the good of the mission, son. After all, there's a maniac on the loose!"

Patrick sighed. "Yeah, I guess so."

"Now duty calls," said SpongeBob. "I'll go that way. Deputy, you go . . . some other way! Roll 'em out!" SpongeBob did his best imitation of a siren as he left. "Wee-oo! Wee-oo! Wee-oo! Wee-oo! Wee-oo! Wee-oo!"

The next thing Patrick knew, a *real* police vehicle pulled up to him.

"Afternoon, son," one cop said to Patrick.

Patrick smiled. "Hello, brothers!" he replied, signaling to his cone hat.

The police officers exchanged puzzled looks with each other. They both wondered what they could possibly have in common with this overstuffed starfish.

Pressing on, one cop said, "We're looking for the maniac."

The other officer stuck a wanted poster in front of Patrick's face and asked, "Have you seen this guy?"

"Aaaaaaaaah!" Patrick screamed. He couldn't believe how horrible and frightening the maniac looked. His eyes were as black as coal. His rectangular, yellow body radiated menace. Patrick couldn't stand it anymore. "Take him away! Take him away!" he shouted.

"Calm down, son!" said one of the officers. "It's just a *drawing*. It's not the real thing."

Patrick breathed a small sigh of relief.

The police officer continued, "Now we're going to show you this drawing of the maniac again and you tell us if you've seen him. Understand?"

"Yeah! Uh-huh!" Patrick replied.

"Okay," said the cop. "Here we go."

"Aaaah! Horrible!" Patrick screamed again. "Take him away!"

The cop quickly took away the drawing. Both officers looked at Patrick and then at each other. Then one of the officers held the drawing up to Patrick again.

"Aaaah!" Patrick shouted.

The officer took away the drawing and Patrick seemed to instantly calm down.

Then the officer showed it to him again.

"Aaaah!" Patrick shouted.

The officer took it away. Patrick was calm. The police officers gave each other a sly look and grinned.

Finally the cops had had enough entertainment for one day and put the wanted poster away.

"Stay *indoors,* son," one cop warned Patrick.

Then the other cop added, "And, uh, take that stupid cone off your head!" Both officers snickered as they drove away.

chapter five

Patrick was spooked. He immediately pulled out his walkie-talkie. "SpongeBob!" he called into it. "SpongeBob, come in! Answer!"

"SpongeBob here. Patrick, report," said SpongeBob.

"I don't want to be a police officer anymore! I'm *scared!*" Patrick cried. "There's a maniac on the prowl!"

SpongeBob tried to calm Patrick down. "Get ahold of yourself, Deputy!"

"Bwaaa! Boo hoo!" sobbed Patrick. "I want to go home!"

Poor rookie, SpongeBob thought sadly to himself. Then through his walkie-talkie he told Patrick, "All right, all right. I'm on my way back."

"Hurry, SpongeBob!" Patrick said. "I think it's getting . . . dark!"

And just like that, it was dark.

"Put on your siren," SpongeBob told Patrick. "I'll be right there."

Patrick shivered with fear as he walked down the street. In a scared voice, he whispered, "Wee . . . woo . . . wee . . . woo . . . wee . . . woo . . ."

Patrick bent down and picked up something. It was a wanted poster for the maniac. When Patrick looked up from the poster, he saw something else—something even scarier. "WEE WOO! WEE WOO! WEE WOO!" he shouted.

In the distance, Patrick *saw* the maniac! Standing under a streetlight, the Maniac looked as scary and dangerous as his picture on the wanted poster.

"SpongeBob!" Patrick cried into his walkie-talkie. "I see him!"

"The maniac?" SpongeBob radioed back.

"Uh-huh!" Patrick responded.

"Where is he, Patrick?" SpongeBob asked.

Patrick looked up at the street signs. "At the intersection of Conch and Coral," he said.

"That's where I am!" declared SpongeBob, getting frightened. "He's right on top of me, but I just can't see him. It's too dark. What's he doing, Patrick?"

Patrick peered into the distance. "Uh . . . he's just standing there . . . *menacingly!*" he

reported. "Get out of there, SpongeBob!"

"Aaaaahhhh!" SpongeBob cried and began running around looking for a place to hide.

In the distance, Patrick heard a horrible cry. He grew even more afraid. "That's his maniac shriek! He's going to attack!" he shouted into his walkie-talkie.

"Patrick, help!" SpongeBob shouted as he ran in circles, growing more and more afraid.

"The maniac's actin' all crazy! RUN!" Patrick instructed.

SpongeBob quickly darted behind a building.

"No! Wait! The maniac's behind that building!" Patrick yelled.

"Yikes!" yelled SpongeBob and hightailed it behind a street sign.

"The maniac just went behind the sign!" Patrick yelled.

SpongeBob ran to a streetlight. He literally picked it up to hide underneath it.

"Wait! Now he's under the streetlight!" Patrick shrieked.

"AAAAAAHHHH!" screamed SpongeBob.

"RUN FOR YOUR LIFE!" Patrick yelled.

SpongeBob was sobbing when he spotted the perfect hiding place. "Aha!" he said and dove headfirst into a mailbox. Among the layers of letters, SpongeBob breathed a sigh of relief.

Suddenly SpongeBob heard Patrick's voice on the walkie-talkie. The walkie-talkie was buried beneath the letters, so the reception wasn't clear.

"Say again, Deputy?" SpongeBob radioed.

"The maniac's in the mailbox!" Patrick repeated.

"YEEOOOWWW!" SpongeBob screamed.

He punched holes in the sides and bottom of the mailbox for his arms and legs. Now wearing the mailbox, SpongeBob began to run, but he couldn't see where he was going. He ran through buildings and homes, trying to get away from the dreaded maniac.

WHAM!

SpongeBob crashed right into a fence. The mailbox split open on impact, and SpongeBob found himself surrounded by the planks of the fence he had just broken through.

"I can't see! I can't see!" he shrieked.

But then SpongeBob opened his eyes and found that there was a piece of paper covering his face. It was one of the wanted posters for the maniac.

"Huh! This guy's not half bad looking for a maniac," SpongeBob thought aloud as he looked at it.

Suddenly SpongeBob saw the resemblance. "Wait a minute, Patrick . . . *I'm* the maniac!"

A line of police officers immediately appeared.

"We'll take *that* as a confession!" declared one officer.

"But . . . I . . . uh . . . ," began SpongeBob.

Just then, Mrs. Puff showed up on the scene. She made her way to SpongeBob. "SpongeBob SquarePants! *There* you are! I turn my back on you for one minute and you destroy half the city. You should be ashamed of yourself!"

"You know this guy?" a cop asked Mrs. Puff.

"Of course I do!" replied Mrs. Puff. "I'm the one who gave him the uniform in the first place. He's *my* responsibility!"

All the police officers narrowed their eyes at Mrs. Puff.

"Uh-oh!" Mrs. Puff said, realizing she had just taken the blame for SpongeBob and all the trouble he had caused. "This is going on your permanent record, SpongeBob!" she called as the police carted her away.

In class the next day, an embarrassed SpongeBob kept to himself. Everyone in Bikini Bottom had heard about his hall monitor fiasco—or had unintentionally been a part of it. As Mrs. Puff finished her lesson for the day, SpongeBob made sure to take precise notes.

"And in conclusion, students," Mrs. Puff said, "red means stop. Green means go. And SpongeBob . . ."

SpongeBob looked up at the TV monitor sitting on top of Mrs. Puff's desk. "Yes, Mrs. Puff?"

"I'd like to see you after class . . . *six months from now!*" snapped Mrs. Puff from her jail cell.

SpongeBob meekly replied, "Yes, Mrs. Puff." He knew now that he had no chance of being hall monitor—*ever again!*

The World's Greatest Valentine

by **Terry Collins**

illustrated by **Mark O'Hare**

based on the original teleplay by Chuck Klein,
Jay Lender, and Merriwether Williams

chapter one

"Happy Valentine's Day, Bikini Bottom!" With this jaunty cry SpongeBob SquarePants sprang out the front door of his pineapple home and ran across the ocean floor.

SpongeBob had thought February 14 would never arrive! His skinny arms were overflowing with valentines of all shapes and sizes. After weeks of waiting, he could deliver his custom-made gifts at last!

"First stop, a valentine for my favorite

next-door neighbor!" SpongeBob said with a happy giggle.

Dancing across the sea grass on the tiptoes of his shiny patent leather shoes, SpongeBob lobbed a large pink valentine into the lap of his frowning neighbor, Squidward.

"Happy Valentine's Day, pal!" SpongeBob sang. "Will you be mine?"

Squidward scowled, then sat back in his outdoor lounge chair. "Why don't you go play in shark-infested waters?" he suggested sarcastically.

"That's a great idea! Sharks need love too, and I've got lots more valentines to give!" SpongeBob replied with a wave. "Good-bye!"

"Good riddance," Squidward said sourly, shredding his valentine into confetti and tossing the pieces over his head.

Spotting Mrs. Puff behind the steering wheel of her blue-and-white motorboat, SpongeBob ran up alongside her vehicle.

"Happy Valentine's Day, Mrs. Puff!" SpongeBob called as he tossed her a red valentine with white lace.

"Oh, my! Thank you, SpongeBob!" the flustered blowfish replied as she opened the valentine.

"I get a bang out of you," Mrs. Puff read, not paying attention to where she was going. . . .

Crunch! Mrs. Puff drove right into a fire hydrant!

Pwooosh! Her body inflated to four times its normal size!

Luckily, Mrs. Puff wasn't injured thanks to her "built-in" air bag!

SpongeBob didn't hear the wreck. He was already dropping off another valentine.

Taking out a pair of tweezers, he selected the smallest paper heart from his pile and held it

out to a tiny green creature with one bulging red eye.

"SpongeBob!" the evil Plankton cried as he looked up. "So, Mr. Krabs has sent you to destroy me! Well, I'm ready for you! Give me your best shot!"

"Okay!" SpongeBob agreed. "Here you go!"

Plankton took the offering and read the note aloud. "I'd walk the plank for you! Be my valentine! Love . . . SpongeBob?"

"Ha-ha-ha-ha!" SpongeBob tittered as he skipped away. "Happy Valentine's Day, Plankton!"

"Curse you, SpongeBob!" Plankton boomed, hopping up and down with anger. "Curse you!"

SpongeBob wasn't listening. He continued dropping off valentines throughout Bikini Bottom. But he had to hurry, for there was a final stop to make before his Valentine's Day was complete. . . .

chapter two

SpongeBob arrived at Sandy Cheeks's underwater treedome. He was ready and eager to take his Valentine's Day plans to the next level.

Sandy was waiting outside in her white diving suit. She had a smile on her face and her hands behind her back.

"Happy Valentine's Day, SpongeBob! I'm nuts for you!" Sandy said with a grin as she handed over a heart-shaped acorn with a twig arrow through the center.

"And I'm bubbles for you, Sandy!" SpongeBob replied, taking out his bubble wand and a bottle of chocolate syrup.

A master of bubble blowing, SpongeBob blew a heart-shaped chocolate surprise to Sandy.

"Mmmm! Mighty tasty!" she said, gobbling up the gift through a portal in her air helmet. "Patrick's going to love the one you made for him!"

Together, SpongeBob and Sandy turned to look at the tremendous chocolate balloon tied down behind the treedome. The balloon was large enough to carry two people in the hanging basket below. There was even a pink marshmallow starfish attached to each side!

"Take me through the plan again," Sandy said as she examined the balloon. SpongeBob dipped the bubble wand into the syrup bottle, took a deep breath, and blew out a floating, three-dimensional chocolate model of the Bikini Bottom Valentine's Day Carnival!

"Step one: Patrick and I get to the Valentine's Day Carnival," SpongeBob said in a commanding tone of voice. "Step two: I position Patrick and myself on top of the Ferris wheel."

"Check and double check," Sandy replied, nodding in agreement. She was amazed at the detail of the chocolate model that hovered in the water.

SpongeBob blew a small bubble replica of the mammoth heart-shaped chocolate balloon. The replica floated over the top of the model carnival. "Step three: You arrive with Patrick's valentine at the designated checkpoint for maximum visual contact."

"Got it!" Sandy agreed, readying herself for take-off.

The small bubble landed on the boardwalk of the chocolate carnival. "Step four: Patrick is thrilled! Mission accomplished!"

"Sounds good, SpongeBob!" Sandy said, untying the ropes that held Patrick's Valentine's Day gift to the bottom of the ocean. "Keep me posted on the shell-phone."

"Right!" SpongeBob replied. "I'll go grab Patrick right now and Operation Valentine will be in full play!"

SpongeBob looked up proudly as Sandy floated away in the balloon. He could hardly wait to see the look on Patrick's face. This was going to be a Valentine's Day his starfish pal would never forget!

chapter three

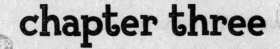

Crunk! Crunk! Crunk! Crunk!

Patrick Star was breaking rocks.

Crunk! Crunk! Crunk!

One rock, actually. He was chipping the stone into the shape of a heart. Patrick knew SpongeBob would be arriving soon, and he wanted to have his gift finished.

Crunk! Crunk!

Patrick loved Valentine's Day almost as much as SpongeBob. The starfish had even bought a new white T-shirt with a red heart on the front for the occasion.

Crunk!

"There!" Patrick said, pleased with his handiwork. "Nice and smooth!"

The starfish lifted the stony valentine just as SpongeBob came up behind him.

"Hi, Patrick!" SpongeBob said.

Patrick looked confused. He peered down at the rock. "Hello?" he said.

"Patrick, it's me. SpongeBob," SpongeBob said.

"Oh, my gosh!" Patrick yelped, dropping the rock in shock. "SpongeBob's stuck inside this rock! Hold on, buddy! I'll get you out!"

Grabbing a second stone, Patrick began to smash the heart-shaped rock. With a series of hammerlike blows, he reduced the valentine to a pile of pebbles!

Patrick was horrified! Had he crushed his best friend?

"SpongeBob?" he whispered, sifting through the remains.

Standing behind Patrick, SpongeBob rolled his eyes. "Yes, Patrick?"

"SpongeBob! Oh, no!" Patrick said, falling to his knees and weeping. He picked up the rubble and held it to his cheek. "My poor pal!"

"Uh, Patrick? I'm right behind you!" SpongeBob said.

Patrick turned and leaped up with delight! "There you are!" he said happily, thrusting out the handful of pebbles. "Happy Valentine's Day! Here's your present!"

SpongeBob took the debris. "Thanks!" he said, then pointed at Patrick. "And I have a present for *you*."

Patrick's eyes widened with excitement!

"You do?" he said. "For *me*!"

"For you!" SpongeBob giggled. "It's the greatest . . . "

Patrick's eyes bulged. He tried to speak, but all he could say was, "Uhhh!"

SpongeBob continued, "The bestest . . . "

A trickle of drool ran down the side of Patrick's mouth. "Yeah?" he said.

"The most fantabulous . . . "

Patrick turned multiple cartwheels with anticipation. "UH-HUH! UH-HUH!"

"The single most amazing present . . . EVER!"

"EEEEEEEEEEE!" Patrick squealed, rolling around on the ocean floor.

"But," SpongeBob added in a teasing tone, "you can't have it yet."

"Huh?" Patrick hopped to his feet and thrust his face into the tip of SpongeBob's long nose. "Why not?" he asked in a hurt voice.

SpongeBob shrugged. "Because it's not ready yet."

Patrick paused for approximately one second. "Is it ready now?" he asked.

"Not yet," SpongeBob teased.

Patrick gritted his teeth. "Now?" he asked hopefully.

"Nope."

"How about now?" he asked.

SpongeBob put his hands on his square hips and frowned. "Do you want to ruin the surprise?" he asked.

"YES!" Patrick said, nodding his head up and down so that the water swirled around his neck like a miniwhirlpool!

"Ah-ah-ah-ahhh!" SpongeBob scolded, wagging a finger.

"Come on, please!" Patrick begged.

SpongeBob crossed his arms. "Sorry."

Patrick fell facedown on the ground. "You gotta tell me!" he pleaded.

"No can do, old chum. You'll just have to wait," SpongeBob said, struggling to move. He looked down at his feet. Patrick had locked both hands onto SpongeBob's right ankle.

"Please, please, please!" Patrick begged, hanging on for dear life as SpongeBob slowly dragged him toward the carnival.

"Uh-uh," SpongeBob said. "You know what they say . . . good things come to those who wait!"

"B-b-but . . . I'm tired of waitin'!" Patrick shrieked. "I want my present now!"

chapter four

SpongeBob glanced at his watch. He was making slower time than anticipated, as Patrick was still clinging to his ankle. He didn't want to be late and miss Sandy's arrival.

"Please! Please! Puh-leeeeze?" Patrick whined.

SpongeBob shook his leg, but his friend had a firm grip. He sighed and kept walking.

"PLEASE! Oh, please tell me! Please! Please?" Patrick begged. "Oh, please you gotta tell me! Tell me! Tell me! Tell me!!! . . . PLEASE!?!"

"Okay, Patrick! Here we are!" SpongeBob finally announced. "One surprise coming up!"

The starfish gazed out across the seascape and gasped. His mouth dropped open and he jumped for joy!

"You got me a carnival!?" Patrick cried happily as he raced through the entrance. "A carnival for me?"

"No, not a carnival, I mean, not exactly. . . ." SpongeBob said, trying to explain. But Patrick wasn't listening.

"Mine! Mine! Mine!" Patrick yelled, glowering at the other Bikini Bottom residents enjoying the attractions. "All right! Everybody out! This is *my* carnival!"

SpongeBob tapped Patrick on the shoulder. "It's not your carnival."

Patrick sagged. "Oh," he said.

SpongeBob dug into a pocket of his square

pants and took out twenty-five cents. "Here," he said, handing the coin to Patrick. "Why don't you take this quarter and—"

"Oh, my gosh . . . a QUARTER!" Patrick cried as he snatched the money from SpongeBob's outstretched hand. "I've always wanted a quarter!"

SpongeBob slapped his soggy forehead. "It's not the quarter," he replied.

"It looks like a quarter."

"It *is* a quarter, but that's not the surprise," SpongeBob explained.

"Oh," Patrick said. "Sorry."

"What I want you to do is take that quarter and buy some cotton candy," SpongeBob said, pointing to a small display cart on wheels. "And then—"

"COTTON CANDY! I can't believe it!" Patrick said, running toward the candy salesman with a wild-eyed look. "Gimme that cart! I'm claiming what is mine!"

The poor salesman ran for his life as Patrick chased him down the boardwalk.

SpongeBob giggled. Patrick was going to be thrilled when Sandy arrived with his surprise!

"Help! Get away! Help me!" the salesman yelled.

"Cotton candy! Gimme!" Patrick replied.

A burst of static erupted from SpongeBob's back pocket. He took out his shell-phone and pressed a button.

"Sandy to SpongeBob . . . come in, SpongeBob!" Sandy's voice crackled from the shell's speaker.

"SpongeBob here."

Onboard the chocolate valentine balloon, Sandy looked out across the ocean and spied the blinking lights and colorful flags of the carnival.

"I've got a visual on the carnival," she said. "You want me to bring 'er in?"

SpongeBob grinned. "Not yet, Sandy. Patrick's still trying to guess what his valentine is!"

Back in the gondola of the balloon, Sandy snickered. "You are such a kidder! Sandy over and out!"

She reached over and adjusted one of the guidelines, letting the chocolate balloon float in place.

Suddenly, she heard a chattering sound!

"Oh, no!" she gasped. A swarm of chomping shellfish was diving straight for the balloon! "Scallops!"

The situation got even worse.

As they got closer, Sandy recognized this particular breed of shellfish. "Chocolate-eatin' scallops!"

chapter five

Tired of chasing the cotton candy cart, Patrick paused in front of SpongeBob. "So, that wasn't my valentine?"

"Nope!" SpongeBob said.

"Then, what? What is it?" Patrick demanded. "I CAN'T TAKE THIS WAITING!"

"You'll have to guess," SpongeBob said with a chuckle.

Patrick ran over and pointed at the "Read Your Fin" fortune-telling tent. "This tent?" he asked.

"Wrong!" SpongeBob said. "You gotta try harder than that!"

Patrick grabbed a very surprised sea bass by the collar. "This guy?" he asked.

"Sorry, no!" SpongeBob said, struggling not to laugh.

Disgusted, Patrick hurled the sea bass away like a javelin and snatched a hotdog from one of the eight hands of an octopus.

"Hey! That's my lunch!" the octopus complained.

"How about this hotdog?" Patrick demanded.

"Tee-hee!" SpongeBob laughed. "Is that your *final* answer?"

Patrick pondered for a few seconds. "Yes," he said.

"No!" SpongeBob replied.

Patrick shoved the hotdog into the owner's mouth and raced over to the Valentine's Day science booth. Hunching over a microscope, he peered into the eyepiece and spotted a swimming creature invisible to the naked eye.

"This paramecium?" Patrick demanded.

SpongeBob held firm. "Sorry, no."

Patrick skidded to a stop and placed a friendly arm around SpongeBob's shoulders. "Heh, heh, heh. You're a sly one," he said with a crazed gleam in his eyes.

Then, the gleam brightened.

Patrick had an idea!

"If I can't find it here at the carnival, then it must be outside on top of . . . Mount Climb-Up-And-Fall-Off!" Patrick cried, racing out of the exit toward the nearby mountain range.

SpongeBob watched his friend grow smaller and smaller in the distance. Patrick ran to the top of the mountain and leaped off with a cry of "AAAAIIIEEE!"

There was a faint *thud* when he landed.

The fall didn't even slow the starfish down. He ran back to SpongeBob.

"The valentine . . . it wasn't there . . . either," Patrick gasped, trying to catch his breath.

SpongeBob's eyes narrowed. "Are you sure?" he asked.

Patrick considered this.

"Dahhh!" he yelled, then turned and ran all the way back to the mountain!

As SpongeBob watched Patrick repeatedly climb up and fall off the tip of Mount Climb-Up-And-Fall-Off, his shell-phone chirped.

"Hello?"

"Sandy to SpongeBob!"

"Roger, Sandy!" SpongeBob said. "You can bring the balloon in now!"

"Um, no can do, SpongeBob," Sandy replied.

Back at the heart-shaped balloon, the

squirrel was using all her kung fu fighting skills to hold the swarm of scallops at bay!

"Why not?" SpongeBob asked.

"We've got ourselves a little problem," Sandy replied, swinging out with a side kick to knock away a hungry shellfish. "Hi-yah! I got a pack of chocolate-eatin' scallops trying to rustle the balloon!"

chapter six

SpongeBob listened in horror. He could hear Sandy grunting with exertion as she battled the attacking scallops!

"Git away, ya sweet-toothed varmints!" she cried. "Hi-yah! SpongeBob, I'm gonna be a little late for the shindig!"

SpongeBob's entire body sagged in his clothes. "Late?" he said worriedly. "But what about—"

"AAAIIIEEE!" Patrick screamed, plunging

once more from the top of Mount Climb-Up-And-Fall-Off.

"Patrick?" SpongeBob finished in a hushed voice.

"Take him up on the Ferris wheel like you planned and I'll meet you there—I hope! Sandy over and out!"

SpongeBob put away the shell-phone. What was he going to do? If Patrick didn't get his valentine, there was no telling what he might do.

"I'm pretty sure it isn't up there," Patrick announced with a wheeze.

"Gahh!" SpongeBob cried in surprise. He hadn't heard his friend come back.

Patrick was a mess. The starfish's new white T-shirt was dirty, his hands were scuffed from the repeated dives, and his face was weary.

"Where . . . is it?" Patrick pleaded, gasping for breath. "Where . . . is . . . my . . . valentine?"

SpongeBob winced, crossed his fingers for luck,

and said, "Actually, it's on the, um, Ferris wheel."

"FERRIS WHEEL!" Patrick bellowed, grabbing SpongeBob by the hand and pulling him toward the brightly lit attraction.

Luckily, there wasn't a line and SpongeBob was able to buy two tickets for the ride. Patrick was entranced as the wheel slowly started to turn. He kept repeating over and over in a whisper, "Ferris wheel, Ferris wheel, Ferris wheel."

As they rose higher and higher, SpongeBob looked around anxiously for Sandy and the chocolate valentine balloon. Unfortunately, he saw nothing but deep blue seawater.

The wheel rotated to a stop. Patrick and SpongeBob were now in the tip-top Ferris wheel car, the highest spot in the carnival.

Patrick turned to SpongeBob. "I'm ready!" he said with a big smile. "I'm ready for the neatest valentine present in the whole wide world!"

"Well, this is where you're gonna get it," SpongeBob replied, pointing directly ahead into the mountains beyond the carnival. "Just keep looking, pal! One present coming right up!"

"Ooooooo!" Patrick said, clapping his hands together with glee. "My valentine is coming!"

While Patrick was distracted, SpongeBob turned away and slipped his shell-phone out of his square pants. "SpongeBob to Sandy," he whispered. "Come in, Sandy! Urgent!"

Back at the balloon, Sandy was in the middle of a terrific brawl! Dozens of chattering scallops were swarming around the two-fisted squirrel and her rich chocolate valentine!

"Sandy to SpongeBob, I got my ox in a ditch over here! Hi-yah!" she cried, placing a well-aimed karate chop at the chin of a hungry scallop. "I'm way off course!"

"How far?" SpongeBob asked. Patrick was

growing more and more restless.

"Beats me, but being lost ain't the problem! These scrunchy ol' scallops are eatin' the balloon!" Sandy replied, punching another shellfish away. "They're everywhere! It's only a matter of time before—"

With those words, one of the scallops broke through Sandy's defenses and bit down hard into the chocolate balloon!

"Aw, shoot!" Sandy groaned.

Air came rushing out of the hole, and the valentine began to drift to the bottom of the ocean.

"We're goin' down, SpongeBob!" Sandy cried. "Switch to Plan B! Switch to Plan B! Sandy over and out!"

"No, Sandy, no!" SpongeBob said. "There is no Plan B! No Plan B!"

The shell-phone was dead. SpongeBob was on his own!

chapter seven

SpongeBob put his shell-phone away before turning to Patrick.

"I don't see it, SpongeBob!" Patrick said in a high-pitched voice. "Do *you* see it? 'Cause I *don't* see it!"

"Uh, well, gee Patrick . . . you know how sometimes you plan something special and things just don't work out?" SpongeBob said nervously.

"No! I don't!" Patrick said, sweat starting to

bead on his forehead. He wiped his brow and turned to SpongeBob. "Holy mackerel! Is it hot up here or what?"

Before SpongeBob could answer the question, Patrick stood up in the Ferris wheel seat. The car shifted, nearly tossing SpongeBob out from beneath the safety restraint bar.

Patrick ripped off his new white T-shirt and threw away the pieces. "Gahhhaa!" he screamed. Scared of falling, SpongeBob tried to wedge himself into the far corner of the Ferris wheel seat.

Patrick began to jump up and down, chanting, "Valentine! Valentine! Valentine!"

From the base of the mighty Ferris wheel to the highest point where SpongeBob and Patrick were perched, the entire carnival ride began to squeak and moan.

SpongeBob's body flapped like a flag in the breeze as he hung on to the safety bar.

"Yaaaaaaah!" he screamed! "Patrick, stop!"

Patrick shook the Ferris wheel even harder. "Val-en-tine! Val-en-tine! Val-en-tine!" he chanted.

"Wait, Patrick, hold it!" SpongeBob cried in sheer terror. He freed one of his hands and waved it at his rampaging pal. "Here it is! I've got your valentine present!"

Patrick froze and turned to look at SpongeBob.

SpongeBob smiled, waggling his fingers. "Eh, hah-ha-ha-ha!" he tittered.

Patrick sat down, and the Ferris wheel stopped shaking. The starfish furrowed his brow and peered at SpongeBob's outstretched hand.

"What's that?" he asked.

"A handshake!" SpongeBob said in his best salesmanlike pitch. "A *friendly* handshake!"

One of Patrick's eyes twitched as he slumped in his seat. He took a deep breath, and then said in a calm voice. "A handshake? *That's* the big gift? You got me a *HANDSHAKE*?!"

SpongeBob reached over and grabbed Patrick's hand and shook it vigorously. "Not just any ordinary ol' handshake! A *friendly* handshake! Happy Valentine's Day!"

As if on cue, the Ferris wheel clanked, and began to lower them to the ground.

Patrick looked at his hand. He didn't say a word, even as his face deflated in disappointment.

Patrick was *not* happy.

"Come on!" SpongeBob said, trying to change the subject as he led Patrick down the boardwalk to the next attraction. "There's lots more stuff to see!"

First there was a visit to the Buddy Bounce,

where SpongeBob happily bounced to and fro like a weightless astronaut on the moon. Patrick also bounced, but his gloomy expression didn't change.

Next was the Wild Mollusk Roller Coaster. SpongeBob and Patrick sat in the front seat and raced around the tracks. SpongeBob screamed and waved, while Patrick stared at his hand and frowned.

Finally, hoping the sights and sounds of the Tiki Fun House would cheer Patrick up, SpongeBob led his friend into the hall of mirrors. SpongeBob giggled as their reflections twisted in comical ways, but Patrick wasn't paying any attention.

SpongeBob sat down on a bench and sighed. How could he make things up to his disappointed pal?

chapter eight

Patrick sat, rubbed his pink chin thoughtfully, and turned to look at SpongeBob.

"I've been thinking," Patrick said in a monotone voice. "At first, a handshake doesn't seem like much, but really, it's the thought that counts."

A tall pink eel slithered up to the bench. She was holding a large heart-shaped box. "Hey, SpongeBob! I just wanted to thank you for this lovely box of chocolates!"

SpongeBob smiled at the eel. "No problem, Fran!"

Patrick frowned, and then continued to speak: "I mean, even though I was expecting more—"

A green fish with an armful of roses strolled up and waved to SpongeBob. "Thanks for the roses, SpongeBob! Happy Valentine's Day!"

SpongeBob sunk down on the bench. "Uh, you too, Dave! Glad you liked them."

Patrick tightened his jaw muscles, and went on, "And not that it matters that we've been friends for so long—"

A blue fish in a yellow dress rode up on a bicycle and stopped next to the bench. She leaned over and said, "Hey, SpongeBob! Thanks for the bike!"

SpongeBob pulled his head down into the collar of his white dress shirt like a

turtle disappearing into his shell.

The blue fish elbowed Patrick and said, "Can you believe this guy? I just met him this morning!"

As she pedaled away, Patrick continued: "So, as I was saying—"

"Excuse me," a new voice said. "Do you guys have the time?"

Patrick whirled on the interloper and grabbed him by the shoulders! Hefting the unlucky guppy over his head, the furious starfish hurled him into the midst of the Happy Valentine's Ring Toss game.

"Yoooaaggghah!" Patrick cried. "PATRICK NEEDS LOVE TOO!"

Patrick beat his chest like a gorilla and ran down the boardwalk into the midst of the carnival, crying in anger and disappointment.

"Oh, no! This is all my fault!" SpongeBob

cried, chasing after his friend. "I've got to try and stop him!"

"AAROOOOOO!" Patrick bellowed. "Where's MY love? Where's the love for Patrick?"

No one was safe! Not the ticket taker, not the soda-pop girl, not even the poor slob wearing the giant red valentine costume and entertaining the kiddies!

"It's an art to have a heart!" the costumed fish sang. "Won't you be mine here in the brine?"

"Yay!" the little fishes replied, wiggling their fins. "We love you, Heartie!"

"Arrrgh! I defy you, heart man!" Patrick screamed, bounding up and scattering the children like scaly bowling pins.

"Run! It's a monster!" the kids cried, fleeing for safety.

Patrick ripped the bright red suit off the poor

entertainer's shoulders, leaving a confused actor standing in his underwear!

A siren began to wail. Over the carnival loudspeaker system, an announcer warned, "Attention, everyone! There's a chubby pink starfish on the loose!"

The panic was on! Everyone ran for the exits! No one wanted to cross an angry starfish!

Especially one that had undergone such a terrible transformation: Patrick's color had changed from pink to purple and his eyes were bloodshot. Pumped up with anger and disappointment, he was now ten times as strong as the average starfish!

He was also ten times as angry.

"Unhappy Valentine's Day, everyone!" Patrick yelled as he ran toward the Swing for Two ride. There were dozens of pairs of swings attached to a tall red-and-white striped pole, and perched on the top was a giant, blinking red heart!

"Heart on stick must die!" Patrick snarled. He wrapped his arms around the base of the pole and strained with all his might to pull it up from the ground!

chapter nine

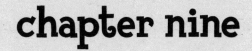

"GWARRR!" Patrick yelled as he struggled to wreck the swing ride.

"No, Patrick! Don't do it!" SpongeBob cried from a safe distance. "I'll make it up to you, I promise!"

Patrick growled, grunted, and pulled as hard as he could, but the mammoth pole wouldn't budge. At last he fell on his butt and put his head in his hands.

"Rooo!" he moaned sadly. "Rooooo!"

A little girl approached Patrick to see if he was okay. She was carrying a red heart-shaped lollipop.

Patrick looked up, spied the lollipop, and once again cried out, "Heart on stick must die!"

Snatching the candy away from the child, the starfish bit the heart-shaped candy off at the tip, chomping and drooling with delight!

SpongeBob stamped his foot. Taking candy from kids was a definite no-no!

"Patrick!" he scolded. "How could you?"

The starfish spun around, his eyes bulging in their sockets and his mouth smeared with red sticky candy. "Mwalughmuhgum!" Patrick snarled. All friendliness was gone, leaving nothing behind but a scaly monster!

"Yikes!" SpongeBob squeaked, fleeing to hide in the midst of the gathering crowd. He was hoping for safety in numbers.

Patrick stood, his arms outstretched, and began to stomp toward the onlookers.

One step forward by Patrick.

One step back by the crowd.

SpongeBob kept his head down, hoping Patrick wouldn't see him.

Patrick picked up the pace and moved closer, his beady eyes seeking out his spongy yellow target.

As one, the crowd shuffled away, trying to maintain their distance from the frustrated starfish. But there was nowhere left for them to go. Patrick had backed them to the end of the dock!

"GRAAAAAH!" the angry starfish yelled. "Give me SpongeB-o-b-b-b!"

The crowd promptly tossed SpongeBob out on his nose.

"Ha-ha-ha-ha-ha!" SpongeBob laughed nervously as he looked up at Patrick. "How's it going?"

"You broke my heart!" Patrick said, waving a fist. "Now, I'm gonna break something of yours!"

SpongeBob got up to his feet and stuck his hands deep in his pockets. "Okay, Patrick," he said sadly. "I know I deserve this!"

"That's right!" Patrick cried. "You deserve it all, 'Mr. Greatest Bestest Most Fantabulous Valentine's Day Present Ever!'"

SpongeBob gestured to the crowd gathered behind him. "I might deserve it, but do they?" Everyone smiled nervously. A few waved their wallets. One lady winked and blew a kiss.

Patrick wasn't buying it. He stomped his foot and bellowed, "They didn't get me anything EITHER!"

A torrent of chocolates, valentines, and presents landed at Patrick's feet.

"Nope!" Patrick said stomping through the pile of gifts. "It's too late for that now! For *all* of you!"

But then, as the angry starfish advanced on the helpless crowd, a new sound rang out across the carnival! A humming noise, like that of a hundred sets of teeth all chattering at once, echoed over the boardwalk!

"Yee-hah! Git along, little shellfish!" Sandy cried, riding atop a repaired, but still intact, heart-shaped chocolate balloon with pink marshmallow starfish on the sides!

With one hand, she cracked a whip. In the other, she held the reins for the now-tamed scallops who were pulling her along!

"Yay! Woo-hoo! Sandy's here!" SpongeBob called. "Valentine's Day is saved!"

chapter ten

"Gallop, you scallops!" Sandy called, expertly maneuvering the balloon. Dropping the reins, she freed the scallops, and the chocolate valentine landed without a sound behind Patrick.

SpongeBob was so excited, he could hardly speak. "Look Patrick! It's here! It's here!" he called. "The best valentine in the whole wide world is right behind you!"

"Su-u-r-r-r-re it is."

"Really!" SpongeBob replied, pointing at the balloon. "See?!"

Patrick crossed his arms and gave SpongeBob a sarcastic grin. "You must think I'm pretty dumb, huh?"

"YES!" the crowd replied in unison.

"Well, I'm not!" Patrick sneered. "I know this is just another trick!"

"But I'm telling you the present is right there!" SpongeBob urged. "Turn around!"

"Nuh-uh!"

SpongeBob stepped closer to Patrick and tried to move him, but the hefty starfish would not budge. "Come on, Patrick!" he begged. "Just turn around!"

"Yeah! Turn around!" someone in the crowd called.

"Nothing doing!" Patrick replied.

"Turn around! Turn around! Turn around!

Turn around!" the crowd chanted.

Patrick was firm. "No, I won't! No, I won't!" he chanted back.

"Turn around! Turn around!"

"You can't make me!"

"Turn! Turn! Turn!"

Patrick hiked up his Bermuda shorts and frowned. "I'm only gonna say this once, and I'm not gonna say it again, so pay attention!" he said. "I am not, I repeat, *NOT,* going to turn around for any reason . . . *EVER!*"

"Howdy, Patrick!" Sandy called from the top of the balloon.

Patrick turned around with a big smile and waved.

"Hi, Sandy!" he replied, before his mouth fell open and hit the wood of the dock with a *ka-clunk.*

There, before his fevered eyes, was the

biggest, most coolest, chocolatey valentine ever! Just like SpongeBob had promised!

"Duh-muh-ba-duh-guh—," Patrick babbled in shock.

SpongeBob slapped him on the back. "Happy Valentine's Day, Patrick!"

"Yay! Yay! Mine! Valentine!" Patrick called as he ran over and embraced the chocolate balloon.

"Awwwwww!" the crowd said, relieved.

Scrambling to get his arms around the balloon, Patrick pressed his face into the chocolate. The valentine smelled delicious! Patrick just had to take one bite!

"Hey, SpongeBob! Is this solid chocolate?" the starfish called, before sinking his teeth into the present.

"Patrick, NO!" SpongeBob cried, but his warning came too late.

The balloon burst with a loud "POP!" covering the entire carnival in a gooey candy mess! Sticky pieces of chocolate valentine and hunks of pink marshmallow were everywhere.

After a moment, Patrick lifted his head. His face was smeared with candy.

SpongeBob's feet appeared nearby, followed by the rest of his body as he wiggled out from under the burst balloon. His head and clothes were coated in chocolate.

Up to their necks in goo, Patrick and SpongeBob looked at each other.

Patrick grinned. "Awwwww, gee, SpongeBob," he said. "You really didn't have to get me anything!"

SpongeBob Superstar

by Annie Auerbach
illustrated by Mark O'Hare

chapter one

"Hey, Patrick!" SpongeBob SquarePants called. "Come look at this!"

Patrick took another lick of his ice-cream cone. "What is it?" he asked, and made his way to his best friend.

"I picked this up at the Krusty Krab as I was leaving," SpongeBob explained and handed Patrick a flyer.

Patrick took the flyer and began to read:

DO YOU WANT TO BE A RICH AND FAMOUS STAR?

DO YOU DREAM OF MAKING IT BIG IN CELEBRITY SEA?

WELL, HERE'S YOUR CHANCE!
SEEKING THE UNDERWATER WORLD'S
BIGGEST DAREDEVIL FOR A TV SPECIAL.
AUDITIONS TOMORROW, 10 A.M.
AT THE KRUSTY KRAB
B.Y.O.S. (BRING YOUR OWN STUNT).

"A daredevil TV show!" exclaimed SpongeBob. "Do you know what this means?"

"Uh . . . must-see TV?" guessed Patrick.

SpongeBob grinned and replied, "Well, of course. But it *also* means we can show off our stunts. We could become famous!"

"But we don't have any stunts," said Patrick.

"Sure we do!" SpongeBob declared. "We just haven't thought of them yet. Hmmm . . ."

"I can . . . I can . . . what can I do?" Patrick wondered.

SpongeBob thought for a moment. He looked at the melting ice cream in Patrick's hand. "You can do something with ice cream!" he told Patrick.

"But how is that a daredevil stunt?" Patrick asked.

"Uh . . . I know! What about the most number of licks it takes to finish an ice-cream cone?" SpongeBob suggested with a smile.

"Yeah!" cheered Patrick. "I'm a daredevil!"

"Well, I'd better go think of a stunt to practice," SpongeBob said. "I'll see you tomorrow."

"See you then!" Patrick called. "I'd better practice, too!" He began to lick and count, "One . . . two . . . three . . ."

SpongeBob went home. After he fed Gary, he took a bath and heated up a leftover Krabby Patty for dinner.

"Ooh . . ." he said, looking at the TV listings while he ate. "There's a *Mermaid Man and Barnacle Boy* marathon on tonight!" Then he remembered he was going to practice a stunt for tomorrow's daredevil auditions. "Well . . . I'll just watch one or two episodes and *then* I'll practice."

chapter two

The next thing SpongeBob knew, light was streaming in through the window. He yawned and rubbed his eyes. "Huh? It's morning already?" he wondered aloud. He saw that the television was still on. A newscaster was reciting the traffic report: "And expect big delays between Coral Boulevard and Anchor Way. Auditions for the World's Biggest Daredevil started at ten o'clock. It seems that everyone in Bikini Bottom is there. Good luck! This is Don Shell reporting . . ."

"Aaaahh!" SpongeBob screamed and sprang

up from the chair. He looked at the clock. "Oh, no! It's already eleven-thirty! I'm late!" He dove into his square pants and ran out the door.

By the time SpongeBob made it to the Krusty Krab, there was a line that seemed to stretch for miles. There were wanna-be daredevils with all sorts of vehicles, gizmos, and gadgets—from inflatable water skis that fit an octopus's eight legs to a pair of stilts made from giant kelp.

"Oh, no! I didn't bring anything!" SpongeBob cried. He squeezed his way through, shouting, "Krusty Krab employee coming through!" He made it inside the Krusty Krab just in time to see Squidward's audition.

"I will be performing my favorite piece, Solitude in E Minor," Squidward announced and began to play his cherished clarinet.

A slimy, stocky fish sitting in a director's chair interrupted him. "Uh, hey! Excuse me?" he said. "Would you tell me how this is a stunt?"

Squidward was instantly offended. "Well, if you must know, it's not actually a stunt," Squidward confessed. "I figured once you heard my brilliant playing, you'd want to make a TV special around *me*."

"Next!" the director called in a gruff voice, his sharp teeth showing.

"You obviously don't know good talent when you see it!" Squidward replied.

"Well, if you get any, let me know," replied the director. Everyone laughed as Squidward slunk away.

SpongeBob put his name on the sign-up sheet and then spotted Patrick.

"I came by your house this morning," Patrick said, "but there was no answer."

"Yeah, I overslept," SpongeBob explained.

"Patrick Star?" an assistant called out.

SpongeBob gave his buddy a thumbs-up sign. Patrick grinned.

"So what stunt are you gonna do?" the director asked Patrick.

"I . . . uh . . . I . . . uh . . . I forget," Patrick replied nervously. He looked over and saw SpongeBob who was making funny faces with his tongue.

Patrick started to giggle. Then he understood what SpongeBob was doing. He looked down at the ice-cream cone in his hand and said, "Oh, yeah! I'm going to do an ice-cream stunt!"

"Oh, boy, this should be good," the director said sarcastically.

"I will attempt the most number of licks it takes to eat this ice-cream cone," explained Patrick. "One . . . two . . ."

Gulp!

"Two licks? What happened?" asked the director.

"Oops! I guess I was hungry," Patrick admitted.

"Well, you'll have plenty of time to eat ice cream—because you won't be on *this* TV special!" the director told him. He looked at his watch. "Everyone take five!"

SpongeBob walked over to Patrick. "Don't

worry about it," he said. "If I get picked and become rich and famous, I promise I'll buy you as much ice cream as you want."

"Thanks!" Patrick replied.

Just then SpongeBob saw his pal, Sandy.

"Howdy, SpongeBob," Sandy said. "Where ya been?"

SpongeBob tried to cover and explained, "Uh . . . I overslept . . . because I was up all night perfecting my stunt."

"Really?" replied Sandy. "I can't wait to see it!"

"Uh, yeah," said SpongeBob. "It should be, uh, interesting. Hey, did you already audition?"

"Sure did!" Sandy said. "I did my best karate tricks. The director really liked me. He said I could be a guest star in the TV special!"

"Way to go, Sandy!" SpongeBob told her.

"The director is still looking for the star, though," Sandy explained. "So you still have a shot!"

"Great!" said SpongeBob. But he knew he'd have to think up a magnificent stunt pretty quickly! "Excuse me, Sandy. I should, uh, go prepare."

"Break a leg!" said Sandy.

SpongeBob looked worried.

"It means good luck," Sandy explained with a laugh.

SpongeBob headed straight for the kitchen. He had to think of a stunt immediately. "Hi, Mr. Krabs," he said to his boss.

"Well, ahoy there, me boy," said Mr. Krabs.

"You're not auditioning, are you?" SpongeBob asked him.

Mr. Krabs laughed. "Oh, no," he said. "I made a deal with the director to use the Krusty Krab for auditions."

"And what do you get in exchange?" asked SpongeBob.

Mr. Krabs pulled out a wheelbarrow of cash. "All of this!" he said excitedly. "I just love those Celebrity Sea types!"

"Mr. Krabs, I need a favor," said SpongeBob.

"Sure, SpongeBob. What is it?" asked Mr. Krabs, counting his money.

"My stunt involves a spatula," SpongeBob explained, quickly looking around, "and Krabby Patties. Can I use the kitchen? Please? Please?"

Mr. Krabs wasn't really listening to SpongeBob. "Uh, sure, SpongeBob . . . seventy-eight dollars, seventy-nine dollars . . ."

SpongeBob grinned. Just then he heard his name being called. He raced out of the kitchen.

chapter three

"SpongeBob SquarePants?" an assistant called out again.

"That's me!" said a cheerful SpongeBob.

"What stunt are you going to perform?" the assistant asked.

"Follow me into the kitchen," SpongeBob said and led the way.

The director looked around at his crew. They were used to directing others, not being directed. Then he grimaced and said, "This better be good."

Once in the kitchen, SpongeBob did his best to

make his stunt sound daring and inventive. He announced, "I'm about to perform a stunt *never* attempted—right before your eyes." Deep down, SpongeBob knew that was really true since he hadn't prepared *anything*. "I shall attempt to make three hundred Krabby Patties in a row."

"How is that a stunt?" someone yelled.

"Boo!" hollered someone else.

SpongeBob noticed the director getting impatient. "You didn't let me finish," he said quickly. "I will perform this daring stunt blindfolded, over a hot-hot-hot grill, *and* with one hand tied behind my back—my Patty-flipping hand!"

"Oooh!" the audience gasped.

Once he was blindfolded and his award-winning flipping hand was tied behind his back, SpongeBob went to work. But because SpongeBob was nervous and he couldn't see what he was doing, he was making Krabby Patties inside out! The bun was on the inside, then the Krabby Patty, mustard, ketchup, pickle, onion, and tomato. The

lettuce was on the outside where the bun should have been!

Everyone started laughing.

"That must be jealous laughter to throw me off," SpongeBob thought to himself, still blind-folded. "I'll just work faster!" Unfortunately, his left hand just couldn't flip as precisely as his right hand, which was still tied behind his back. Soon he was flipping Krabby Patties all over the place.

The director and his crew all covered their heads. It seemed to be raining Krabby Patties!

Just then Mr. Krabs walked in. "What the barnacle!" he cried. "Me kitchen! Me Krabby Patties!" He ran over to SpongeBob who was buried beneath a pile of Krabby Patties and took off his blindfold.

By this time, everyone was hysterical—even the director. He didn't know which was funnier: the stunt or SpongeBob himself. He pulled his production team close to him. "Forget the daredevil stunt show," he whispered with a sinister laugh. "I've got an idea that will make us millionaires! We're going to turn this show into a rip-roaring blooper show. We'll be the funniest thing on television!"

The director called SpongeBob over. "Hey, kid, what's your name?"

"SpongeBob SquarePants," replied the harried fry cook.

The director stuck his fin out. "I'm Cuda. Barry Cuda," he said.

"It's an honor, sir," SpongeBob replied, shaking his fin.

"How would you like to be a star?" the director asked SpongeBob.

"Me?" asked SpongeBob.

"That's right. You're the next daredevil superstar!" Barry Cuda assured him. "There won't be an invertebrate in Bikini Bottom who won't want to be in your shoes!"

"Woo-hoo!!" SpongeBob exclaimed.

Barry immediately saw that SpongeBob was

easily influenced. "That will make it easier to get him to do what I want," he muttered to himself. Then he pulled out a floor-length contract and said, "Okay, let's make a deal!"

SpongeBob couldn't believe it. "I'm going to be a star! SpongeBob SquarePants is gonna be a *star*!" he said dreamily to no one in particular.

"That's right," Barry assured him. "A star is born! In fact, just like a real star, I think you need a stage name—how about SpongeBob Superstar?"

SpongeBob practically jumped for joy as he signed the contract—with his new celebrity name.

"Everyone go home!" Barry Cuda announced. "We've found our star!"

SpongeBob beamed. He ran over to his friends and excitedly said, "Can you believe it? *Me!* He picked little ol' *me* to be the star!"

"Way to go, little square dude!" Sandy told him.

"That's me boy!" Mr. Krabs said, patting him on the back.

"I just can't believe it!" SpongeBob shouted.

"Wow!" cried Patrick. "I know a *real* superstar! Can I touch you?"

SpongeBob stuck out his hand and grinned. "*Almost* a superstar. But when I become rich and famous, I promise I'll share everything with you!"

Squidward, though, was still annoyed about the clarinet incident and said, "Well, at least you won't be working *here* for a while."

"Oh, no! I forgot!" SpongeBob exclaimed. "Mr. Krabs, is it okay if I take some time off to tape this special?"

"Absolutely!" Mr. Krabs replied. "I'm sure Squidward won't mind covering your shifts," he added with a belly laugh.

"Argh!" Squidward groaned.

Barry Cuda approached SpongeBob and told him, "Shooting starts tomorrow morning."

"Oh, Mr. Cuda," began SpongeBob, "these are my friends."

"Yeah, whatever," said Barry. "See you tomorrow."

"Should I practice any stunts?" asked SpongeBob.

"NO!" Barry said a little too quickly. "I mean, uh, no, it's not necessary."

"Okay, Mr. Cuda," SpongeBob replied cheerily. "See you tomorrow!"

chapter four

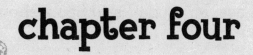

The next day SpongeBob woke up bright and early. He was so excited. "Superstar! Superstar!" he sang eagerly as he left his pineapple house.

The first stunt was to take place in Oyster Bay. The set was buzzing with activity everywhere SpongeBob looked. Set decorators were dressing up the set. Lighting technicians were adjusting lights. Costumers were putting the finishing touches on costumes.

"So this is what showbiz is all about," SpongeBob said in awe.

Barry, the director, spotted the one-of-a-kind creature who was going to make him a millionaire. "SpongeBob! Come over here, kid. Time for makeup and wardrobe," Barry told him.

"Aye, aye, Mr. Cuda!" said SpongeBob with a salute.

"Call me Barry," the director told him.

"Aye, aye, Barry!" SpongeBob replied.

Three long hours later, SpongeBob was ready. The daredevil costume originally designed wasn't made for a sponge—let alone a square one. Needless to say, a lot of sewing took place that morning.

Finally SpongeBob emerged wearing a pair of square trunks and a matching cape, and holding a shiny helmet. "I don't know," he worried, pointing to the costume. "Is it really me?"

"Maybe not," replied Barry. "But it *is* SpongeBob Superstar!"

"Oh, yeah!" agreed SpongeBob, his eyes lighting up.

SpongeBob's first stunt involved trying to get the rare black pearl from the granddaddy of all oysters, The Big Kahuna.

When SpongeBob was first told of this stunt he said, "Seems easy enough! I'm sure that Mr. Kahuna won't mind if I borrow his pearl." What SpongeBob didn't realize was what he'd have to go through to retrieve the pearl. With a bright red skateboard, SpongeBob was supposed to skate on a track through the oyster bed. The track leading up to the prized pearl was full of nail-biting turns, extreme loop-de-loops, and hair-raising drops! As if that weren't scary enough, swimming below the oyster bed were twenty electric eels!

After SpongeBob found out what he was supposed to do, his eyes popped out of his head. Once he recovered, he cried, "I'm gonna do what?" his head shrinking slightly in fear.

"Everyone's gotta start somewhere," Barry reminded him.

"But what about those eels?" SpongeBob asked. "One electric shock and I'll . . . I'll . . . I'll be all dried up!"

"You can do it, kiddo," Barry urged him. "This is your first step toward stardom, remember?"

SpongeBob's head swelled up a bit and he grabbed his helmet. "You're right. Let's do it!"

Barry wouldn't let SpongeBob do any practice runs, stating that he wanted to capture the excitement and drama of doing it for the very first time.

Once SpongeBob was in place, Barry yelled, "Action!" and the cameras started to roll.

SpongeBob started skateboarding down the track and completed the first turn. Unfortunately, it was feeding time for the electric eels, and SpongeBob looked like the perfect lunch to them.

"Stay back! Stay back!" SpongeBob shouted at the eels. "You wouldn't like me anyway! I'm kind of chewy!" But the eels were still coming at him. He started to skate even faster. Then, on a loop-de-loop, something caught his eye inside one of the oysters. It was the most beautiful black pearl he had ever seen.

Crash! Boing! Boing! The skateboard went flying off the track as SpongeBob fell and bounced off a row of oysters.

"Whoa!" SpongeBob yelled as he tumbled up and around, the eels nipping at him along the way. Finally he ended up headfirst inside of an oyster—the one that held that precious black pearl. "I've got it!" he mumbled.

"Cut!" yelled Barry.

Luckily, SpongeBob was just out of reach of the eels, but with only his feet sticking out of the oyster, he was still worried. That certainly *wasn't* the way the stunt was supposed to go, was it?

After the production crew rescued SpongeBob, Barry rushed right over to him and raved, "Fantastic!"

"Huh?" said SpongeBob.

"You really nailed it, kid," Barry told him.

"But I wasn't supposed to—" began SpongeBob.

"Eh, don't worry about it. That was better than we could have ever planned!" Barry declared and signaled his crew.

"Uh . . . gee, thanks," SpongeBob said hesitantly.

The crew surrounded SpongeBob and applauded. "That was great! You're so brave! You're a star!" they all cooed.

SpongeBob shrugged. "Well, maybe it wasn't as bad as I thought," he said, and again his head swelled up a little.

On his way home, SpongeBob ran into Patrick.

"How was your first day?" Patrick asked excitedly.

"It was incredible!" exclaimed SpongeBob. "I think I might be a natural at this daredevil stuff!"

"Holy sea cow!" cried Patrick. "My best friend's a daredevil star!"

All the way home, Patrick and SpongeBob planned what they'd do when SpongeBob became a big star.

chapter five

The following day, SpongeBob's daredevil stunts were to take place in Goo Lagoon. This time, SpongeBob wasn't afraid. He was ready to take on whatever stunts were assigned. After going through makeup and wardrobe, he sat and waited while final technical adjustments were made.

"SpongeBob, me boy!" a voice said.

SpongeBob jumped up. "Mr. Krabs!"

"I came to see how you're holding up," Mr. Krabs said. "I even brought you some Krabby Patties."

SpongeBob took a step back and replied, "Not

for me, thanks. I'm on a strict diet. A superstar's diet. No Krabby Patties allowed."

"Why, that's crazy!" Mr. Krabs exclaimed.

"It's a sacrifice we stars *must* make," SpongeBob said snootily. It was hard for him to concentrate, though, with the scent of Krabby Patties wafting through the air. They sure were tempting!

Mr. Krabs looked puzzled. "All right, lad, if you say so," he said. Then he quickly left because he suddenly felt out of place.

Barry came up to SpongeBob. "Ready for today's stunts?" he asked.

"You bet!" SpongeBob declared. Then after a moment he asked, "Uh, Barry? What *are* today's stunts?"

"They'll be a snap for you. Why, with your talent—and that face—I see big things in your future, SpongeBob! Now come on, surf's up!"

SpongeBob imagined his life in Celebrity Sea. All the money he could want, surrounded by adoring fans, getting asked for autographs . . .

His daydream was interrupted as he found himself being carried over to a surfboard. "Huh? I don't surf," SpongeBob said and looked around him.

"Aaahh!" he suddenly yelled. He was indeed on a surfboard. But he learned that he was supposed to surf on one foot, juggle ten plates, balance a stack of coral on his head, *and* balance a spoon on his nose—all at the same time!

"This isn't surfing!" he objected.

"Sure it is! It's surfing—SpongeBob Superstar-style!" replied Barry.

Before SpongeBob could protest any further, he was pushed out to Goo Lagoon by the production crew.

In typical SpongeBob fashion, the stunt didn't go at all the way it was meant to. A big wave swelled and SpongeBob panicked.

Crash! Splash!

Everything he was trying to balance went flying in different directions.

"Yikes!" he yelled. The enormous wave was

coming right at him. Not knowing what else to do, SpongeBob decided to try bodysurfing instead. He dropped onto his stomach and started to paddle with his hands. He felt like he was getting sucked into the wave so he began to paddle even faster. In fact, SpongeBob was paddling so fast that his arms became a whirlwind of motion, like propellers on an airplane. He desperately hoped that it would help save him.

But the only thing it did was cause the big wave to swell up even more, until it was almost a tidal wave!

"Whoa!" shouted SpongeBob as he actually began surfing the wave.

"Now that's what I call surfing!" an assistant remarked.

"And that's what I call comedy!" said Barry. "Keep rolling!"

Splash!

SpongeBob, the surfboard, and tons of water washed up onto the shore.

Barry didn't care. He couldn't have imagined a funnier stunt if he had thought of it himself! He whispered to his crew, "Make sure you help feed his ego." Then he approached SpongeBob. "What a star performance that was! You're great, kid!" Barry told him.

Once again, SpongeBob's head swelled up a bit. "Yeah, maybe I am . . ." He noticed the round of applause he was getting. Then his head swelled even more. "Yes! Yes! I *am* great!"

"We're losing light," said Barry. "Does our Superstar need a break, or can he do one more?"

"I'm ready! I'm ready!" SpongeBob declared, his head growing even larger.

"Excellent," said Barry. "Now where's that squirrel?"

Sandy came on to the set and announced, "Here I am, Mr. Cuda. I'm ready for my close-up."

"Very funny," Barry said with a sneer. "Now, this next stunt involves karate—"

"Oh, wow! I love karate!" SpongeBob

exclaimed, and he pulled out his safety gear. "Safety first!" He noticed his helmet was a little tighter than usual, but he could still squeeze it on.

"Hi-yah!" Sandy shouted, striking a position.

"Wah!" yelled SpongeBob with a spin.

SpongeBob and Sandy loved to practice karate. Barry tried his best not to get annoyed. After all, if his TV show was a success, he could retire to the hills of Celebrity Sea and spend his time counting his millions. "My little stars, why don't you save it for the camera, hmmm?"

Finally SpongeBob and Sandy were poised and ready for combat. They were to fight each other while jumping across dangerous Rock Falls. Rock Falls was made up of separate pieces of rock, each with a one-thousand-foot drop. One slip and it was into the wild blue yonder.

"Action!" called Barry.

"Prepare for a long, merciless whopping!" Sandy said confidently.

"That'll be the day!" SpongeBob replied.

"Hi-yah!" yelled Sandy as she did a powerful jump kick. She landed on SpongeBob's rock.

But SpongeBob was quick on his feet. He pulled out his best move: a double overhand squirrel-knot.

Sandy blocked it and jumped to another rock. "Nice try, Sponge Brain!" she said with a laugh.

Soon it became clear that Sandy was winning, which was unacceptable to SpongeBob. "After all, *I'm* the star," he said to himself.

As a last resort, SpongeBob used the best defense he could. With all his might, he took his huge head and pummeled Sandy with it. SpongeBob's head was now so large that it nearly threw him off balance—and off the steep rock!

Sandy seemed to be down when suddenly she squirmed out from underneath SpongeBob's head. With a loud "Wah!" she delivered a lethal knuckle punch.

SpongeBob flipped over and ended up facedown with his head wedged between two rocks.

"Cut!" yelled Barry. "Great job, you guys!"

Once SpongeBob was back on his feet, he pulled Sandy aside. He was very upset. "Did you *have* to do that last move?" he hissed. "You made me look bad out there!"

Sandy couldn't believe what she was hearing and quickly blurted out, "You didn't need me to help you look like a fool. You did that all by yourself. I won fair and square."

"It's not cool to steal the star's spotlight," SpongeBob said bitterly.

"I thought we were partners," said Sandy, "but I guess with your new stardom, there's not enough room for me. See ya, SpongeBob."

SpongeBob sighed. Sandy was one of his favorite pals. However, there wasn't much time to feel bad as Barry rushed over.

"What's the matter?" Barry asked.

"Sandy and I had a fight," SpongeBob explained. "I can't believe how stupid she made me look out there."

"Stupid? What are you, crazy?" replied Barry. "You were terrific, kid! Wait until you see the footage. *Trust me.*"

SpongeBob had no reason not to trust Barry. As his head swelled some more, he shrugged and said, "Sandy just doesn't understand show business, I guess."

"That's right! Tomorrow we'll shoot the last stunt. I'll see you then, Superstar," Barry called over his shoulder as he walked away.

"I'll be there!" SpongeBob promised.

chapter six

The next day when SpongeBob walked on to the set, he made a few heads turn. By now he was used to this, for he was a big star. He had already hired a press agent, a driver, and a personal secretary.

This time, however, heads were turning because SpongeBob's head had now swelled to epic proportions. Someone hesitantly pointed out the bizarre big-head phenomenon to Barry. But instead of getting mad, Barry just grinned. He quickly called a crew meeting.

"Now listen," he told everyone, "it appears

that SpongeBob's head is actually growing because of his big ego. I think his huge head will make this TV show even better. But we don't want him to become worried about it—you know how actors can be. So just act as if nothing's wrong."

"Sure!" replied the crew.

SpongeBob came out of the makeup and wardrobe departments feeling quite good about himself.

Barry began to explain to SpongeBob what the final stunt was. "Okay, Superstar, this is the most dangerous stunt yet. Only a *true* daredevil could pull it off."

"Bring it on!" declared SpongeBob. "I'm unstoppable!"

"Great! How do you like paddle bikes?" asked Barry.

"Love 'em!" SpongeBob exclaimed, though he had never been on one in his life.

"You are going to do a stunt that will not only be the most significant stunt for the TV show, but will surely put you in the record books, too!"

"All right!" SpongeBob cheered. "Hey, do I get paid extra for that?"

"Uh . . . we'll talk about that later," Barry said. "Now get on that paddle bike, Superstar, and let's make TV history!"

Sitting high atop a paddle bike at the edge of Jellyfish Fields, SpongeBob was supposed to ride down a ramp and jump over twenty-five boats lined up in a canyon below.

SpongeBob tried to put on his helmet, but it seemed to be way too small. After a few minutes of pushing and squishing, he barely got it around his head. He signaled to the crew that he was ready to go and the cameras began to roll. SpongeBob confidently started down the ramp.

Suddenly his helmet snapped off and fell over the edge of the ramp. "Oh, no!" SpongeBob worried. But soon he'd be worrying about something else.

Buzz . . . buzz . . . buzz . . .

"What's that sound?" Barry wondered.

Buzz . . . buzz . . . buzz . . .

SpongeBob was gaining speed.

BUZZ . . . BUZZ . . . BUZZ . . .

The entire crew looked up in horror. Following SpongeBob down the ramp was a huge group of jellyfish! The leader appeared to be wearing a helmet—the helmet SpongeBob had dropped!

BUZZ . . . BUZZ . . . BUZZ . . .

SpongeBob finally looked behind him. "Yeeooooww!" he shrieked, and lost his balance.

Screech!

The paddle bike went careening off the ramp and into the canyon. Flying through the air, SpongeBob separated from the bike and landed in one of the boats below. Luckily, his huge head cushioned the fall! SpongeBob turned himself right side up in the boat, put his foot on the gas, and floored it. He raced through the area, still followed by a gang of angry jellyfish.

"Ow! Ow!" cried the crew members as they were stung by the jellyfish.

But with only his career on his mind, Barry ordered, "Keep rolling!"

SpongeBob steered the boat out of the canyon, hoping he would lose the jellyfish. But they followed him all the way through Goo Lagoon and even into Bikini Bottom, stinging everyone along the way. To make matters worse, SpongeBob still didn't have his driver's license, so he was hitting nearly everything in his zigzagging path.

Finally SpongeBob was able to circle around and end up back in Jellyfish Fields. Just then, he had an idea. He called to Barry, "Play some music! It's our only chance!"

Someone quickly turned on a boom box and suddenly the jellyfish became calmer and all moved to the beat of the music.

"Cut! That's a wrap!" called Barry. "Thank you everyone!"

No one reacted with the joy normally experienced at the end of a TV shoot. Instead, they were all groaning and nursing their painful stings.

As SpongeBob got out of the boat, he noticed that he had survived with no stings at all. "I guess that's my protective star-coating," he said to himself. "I knew I was a natural daredevil."

"SpongeBob!" called a voice.

SpongeBob whirled around to see Patrick standing there. "Did you see it, Patrick? Did you see that amazing stunt?"

"Uh-huh!" replied Patrick. "*Everyone* in Bikini Bottom did! The hospitals are overflowing!"

"I'm glad they all could be a part of my rising success," said SpongeBob.

Patrick was about to ask SpongeBob what he meant when Barry came over.

Barry looked at Patrick and said, "Well, well, well, if it isn't the ice-cream king." He snickered and looked at SpongeBob to join in.

SpongeBob laughed too, which surprised Patrick. Why would his best friend laugh at him, he wondered.

"Well, Superstar," Barry said, "I'll see you at

the premiere. Invite whoever you want."

"Wow! My first premiere!" gloated SpongeBob.

"Hey, SpongeBob, why don't we celebrate?" suggested Patrick. "We could go get ice cream or something."

SpongeBob scoffed. "I don't have time for those trivial things," he told Patrick. "I've got interviews to give, people to meet, places to go . . ."

"But what about all the plans we made for when you were a big star?" Patrick said, feeling hurt.

But SpongeBob didn't notice. "Uh, yeah . . . we'll do lunch. Have your secretary call my secretary," he replied snottily.

"But I don't have a secretary!" called Patrick as SpongeBob walked out, talking on his new shell phone.

chapter seven

Finally it was the night of the TV special world premiere. Besides being broadcast oceanwide, Barry had rented out a theater for a celebrity-filled screening. It was a star-studded event! Stars and celebrities from far and deep showed up, including actor Albert Albatross, comedian Lainie Angelfish, famed writer Harriet Herring, and the always magnificent Catfish van Damsel. Even Lady Beluga was there with her stunning daughter, Caviar!

By this time, SpongeBob's ego was so big that he could hardly fit his head through the door. He was so excited to be seeing his name and sponginess on-screen. SpongeBob walked down the red carpet, and photographers snapped his picture as he posed and signed autographs. He was more than ready to embrace his fans and his newfound stardom as a famous daredevil.

Inside the theater, the screening was about to begin. SpongeBob looked around. All the seats he had saved for his friends were empty. "Where could they be?" he wondered. He knew his secretary had sent out invitations to all the little people in Bikini Bottom.

"I'm sure they'll be here soon," SpongeBob said. Eventually the lights dimmed and his friends still weren't there. "Well, their loss," he mumbled, trying to convince himself.

The music cued up and a voice-over was heard: "From the famous fish that brought you *When Anchovies Attack II,* comes the first in a series of daredevil specials." A title graphic flashed on the screen.

SpongeBob's eyes bugged out. The TV special was no longer called *Underwater World's Biggest Daredevil.* It was changed to *Underwater World's Biggest Goofball!*

The director had tricked him! Watching the first stunt, SpongeBob slumped down in his seat. It was no longer a TV special about daredevil stunts, but about stunts gone hysterically wrong. He had made such a fool of himself! Totally embarrassed, SpongeBob's swollen head actually began to shrink.

SpongeBob could only bear to watch about half of the show. Completely humiliated, he slunk out of his seat and out of the theater.

As SpongeBob walked through the streets of Bikini Bottom, he passed houses where families were watching the TV special. He could hear them roaring with laughter and his head shrank some more.

Up ahead, SpongeBob spotted the Krusty Krab. He felt a glimmer of hope. He rushed up to

the window and pressed his face against the glass. "Hey! What are all my friends doing here? They were supposed to be at my premiere. Well, only one way to find out," he said and went inside.

From all the laughter, it seemed that everyone was having a pretty good time. SpongeBob quickly looked around to see if it was because of his embarrassing TV show, but he didn't see a television. They just seemed to be having fun.

"Hi, everybody!" SpongeBob shouted.

But no one answered him.

"Wasn't that a great day at Goo Lagoon today?" Patrick said to Sandy.

"It sure was!" declared Sandy.

"You went to Goo Lagoon without me?" SpongeBob asked Patrick. But Patrick just turned the other way.

"Mr. Krabs, that was the best Krabby Patty I've ever had," Squidward stated.

"Are there any Krabby Patties left?" asked SpongeBob, feeling quite hungry.

Mr. Krabs just ignored him and said, "Why, thank you, Squidward! Just for that, remind me to give you a promotion."

Squidward's eyes lit up and he replied, "Uh, Mr. Krabs? Give me a promotion."

The group broke out into hysterical laughter.

"Ha ha ha ha!" SpongeBob joined in.

Suddenly everyone else became quiet. SpongeBob's head shrank some more.

"In fact, I think there's an opening for a fry cook," Mr. Krabs continued.

"Wait!" SpongeBob cried. "That's *my* job!"

Still, no one was listening to him.

"Remember the good ol' days when SpongeBob was the fry cook?" asked Patrick.

"Yeah," agreed Squidward. "Now he's just a legend in his own mind."

Everyone chuckled. By this time, SpongeBob's head not only had shrunk back to its normal size, but it had begun to shrink even smaller. Defeated, he headed into the kitchen and began to sob.

"What have I done?" he moaned. "I've made a fool of myself on oceanwide TV *and* lost all my friends." He dabbed his eyes with some seaweed. "No TV deal is worth losing all of this. I don't belong in Celebrity Sea; I belong right here in Bikini Bottom!"

Brrrriinngggg!

SpongeBob's shell phone was ringing. "Hello?" he said sheepishly.

It was Barry Cuda. He was *not* happy. "Where are you, kid? Why aren't you *here?*"

SpongeBob began to sob again. He squeaked out, "I'm at the Krusty Krab."

"I'll be right there," Barry told him.

A few minutes later, Barry burst through the front door of the Krusty Krab. He didn't greet anyone. He just demanded, "Where's Superstar?"

SpongeBob's friends hated that name. With hisses, they all pointed to the kitchen.

"I'm sorry, Barry," SpongeBob said when Barry came into the kitchen.

"Sorry ain't gonna cut it, Superstar," said Barry. "You're under contract. You *have* to talk to the press and go to the parties. I thought that this was what you wanted!"

SpongeBob mustered up all his courage and said, "I wanted you to make me a star—not a fool!"

"Hey, come on. This is show business, kid," Barry said. "It's a fish-eat-fish world out there."

"Well, I'm *not* a fish and I want out of your fish-eat-fish world," SpongeBob declared. "I want to go back to my normal life—where I can be with my friends, and go jellyfishing, and go bubble blowing—"

Like the sleazy director he was, Barry whipped out the contract SpongeBob had signed. "Don't make me show my teeth, Superstar," said Barry. "You're all mine for the next ten years."

"What?" exclaimed SpongeBob. "Let me see that!" He grabbed the contract and read the really, really, really fine print. He sighed and said, "Uh-oh."

Just then SpongeBob's friends burst into the kitchen. They had overheard the entire conversation. Even though SpongeBob had been annoying lately, they sure weren't going to let this barracuda bully him.

"Let me see that contract," said Mr. Krabs. "Hmm . . . very interesting . . ."

"What?" Barry said, growing impatient.

"This contract is between you and SpongeBob Superstar," Mr. Krabs explained. "But there's no one here by that name."

"He's standing right there," said Barry, pointing to SpongeBob.

"No, I'm SpongeBob *SquarePants,*" SpongeBob corrected him.

"So this contract isn't legal," Mr. Krabs pointed out.

"But . . . but . . ." began Barry, getting very frustrated. "This is not the end of this. I'm talking to my lawyers!" Then he stormed out.

"I just hate those Celebrity Sea types!" Mr. Krabs declared.

SpongeBob felt grateful and gushed, "You guys didn't have to come and rescue me—but I'm *so* glad you did!"

"We knew you needed help," said Sandy.

"I think you needed rescuing from yourself," Squidward said.

"Yeah, I guess I did get a little out of control, huh?" said SpongeBob.

Everyone just stared at him.

"Okay, okay, I got *a lot* out of control," he admitted. "I'm really sorry."

"That's okay. You're forgiven," everyone told him.

"I can't believe I was going to give up *all* this for a life in Celebrity Sea," said SpongeBob.

"All what?" asked Patrick.

"All of my good friends," answered SpongeBob.

"And Krabby Patties!" added Mr. Krabs. He handed SpongeBob a spatula. "Welcome back, SpongeBob! It hasn't been the same without you."

"It's good to be home," said SpongeBob and he fired up the grill. He was happy to be back and happy his head was back to its normal square size—just the perfect size.

SpongeBob SquarePants

Sandy's ROCKet

by **Steven Banks**

illustrated by **Clint Bond**

chapter one

SpongeBob SquarePants was running as fast as he could to Sandy Cheeks's house.

It was a beautiful day in Bikini Bottom and SpongeBob couldn't wait to see his friend. He wanted to show her a new karate move he had seen on TV.

"Hey, Sandy!" he yelled as he knocked on her door. "Open up, I . . ." Suddenly SpongeBob stopped knocking. He looked up and saw something next to Sandy's house. It made him forget all about the new karate move.

It was a rocket ship!

It was enormous. It was taller than Sandy's house. SpongeBob had to lean so far back to see the top that he fell over.

The rocket ship was painted red and silver. It had a point at the top and there were little windows on the side.

Sandy opened her front door. "Howdy, SpongeBob! How do you like my rocket ship?"

"Wow!" said SpongeBob.

"Let's go inside and I'll show you around," said Sandy, opening the door of the rocket ship.

"What are you going to do with it?" asked SpongeBob.

"I'm going to the moon!" said Sandy as they went inside.

SpongeBob's eyes opened wide. His heart began to beat fast. "The moon! Wow! Can I go?"

Sandy shook her head. "No way, SpongeBob! Remember what happened when you went with me to find The Lost City of Atlantis?"

"I forget," said SpongeBob.

"We found it and then you lost it!" said Sandy. "Besides, there's not enough room for you in my rocket ship."

"But I don't take up that much space," said SpongeBob as he squished himself down as small as he could get. "See?"

Sandy shook her head. "Sorry, SpongeBob. You can't go."

SpongeBob opened up a tiny drawer and squeezed inside it. "Wait, look! I can fit in here!" he called.

"I need that drawer for important scientific papers," said Sandy.

SpongeBob popped out of the drawer and looked around the rocket ship.

"How about in here?" asked SpongeBob as he jumped inside a test tube.

"I need that test tube, too," replied Sandy.

SpongeBob climbed inside a juice bottle. "I could stay in here," he said.

"No you can't!" cried Sandy. "SpongeBob, this is an important scientific mission! I don't have time for fun and games!"

"I do!" said SpongeBob as he popped out of the juice bottle.

"No games! And no stowaways either!" said Sandy.

SpongeBob saw a little cupboard with bars in the front. It looked like a little jail. He quickly climbed inside. "Fine! Put me in the brig! Lock me in irons! I don't mind! I just wanna go to the moon!"

Sandy pulled SpongeBob out. "That's my air vent, SpongeBob! I need that, too!"

SpongeBob got down on his knees. "Oh, please can I go to the moon? Can I? Can I? Please-please-please?"

Sandy sighed. She could always use an extra hand. And SpongeBob was fun to have around.

"All right!" she said. "You can ride in the cargo hold, as long as you don't act crazy!"

SpongeBob jumped up and began running around the rocket ship as fast as he could. "I'm going to the moon! I'm going to the moon! Moon ride! Moon ride! Fly me to the moon!"

Sandy grabbed him. "Hey! Be careful! Don't touch anything!"

SpongeBob immediately picked up a long tube that had a trigger and a net at the end. "Wow! Look at this popgun! Are we gonna go hunting aliens on the moon?"

"Aw, hush, silly!" said Sandy. "This is for

harvesting moon rocks. Come on, I'll show you."

They walked out of the rocket ship.

Sandy aimed the moon rock harvester at some faraway rocks. She pulled the trigger and little nets shot out and wrapped themselves around the rocks.

"See? That's how I can collect moon rock specimens," said Sandy. "I've even got an extra one that you can use."

"Great! But when we're done playing with the rocks, we can use it for some serious alien hunting, right?" asked SpongeBob.

Sandy sighed. "Aliens? Are you nuts? I've been to the moon. There are no aliens."

SpongeBob smiled and chuckled quietly. "Sandy, Sandy, Sandy. How can you be so unscientific? There's evidence of aliens all around us! How do you explain cooties?

Cowlicks? Ninety-nine-cent stores?"

Sandy shook her head. "SpongeBob, you don't know the first thing about outer space. Now go home and get some shut-eye. Be here tomorrow at the crack of dawn. And leave your crazy alien ideas behind!"

chapter two

SpongeBob immediately went home to his pineapple house and climbed into bed.

Gary, his pet snail, was on the floor next to SpongeBob's bed. Gary slept on a pile of newspapers just in case he had an accident. He wasn't pineapple-house-trained yet.

SpongeBob set his alarm clock for the crack of dawn. He tried to go to sleep, but he was so excited, it wasn't easy. He stared at his clock. He had *hours* to go before dawn.

"Hurry up!" he said to the alarm clock. "Go faster!"

The alarm clock paid no attention and kept on slowly ticking.

SpongeBob looked out his window. It was still dark. "Come on, crack of dawn—start cracking!"

Just then Patrick Star, SpongeBob's best friend, popped his head in the bedroom window. "Hiya, SpongeBob! I heard you were going to the moon with Sandy."

"I am. And I'm trying to go to sleep!" replied SpongeBob.

"I have to ask you a very important question," said Patrick as he climbed through the window. "Is Sandy's rocket safe from aliens?"

"There *are* no aliens," said SpongeBob. "Just ask Sandy . . . Little Miss Smarty-pants Scientist."

"Oh, really?" said Patrick as he held up a

brown paper bag. "Well, then I guess you won't be needing this can of Mr. Funny Ha-Ha's Alien Repellent Spray!"

"Mr. Funny Ha-Ha's Alien Repellent Spray!" cried SpongeBob, grabbing the bag. "Let me see that!"

SpongeBob pulled out a bright red spray can and read the label: "GUARANTEED TO KEEP ALL ALIENS AWAY! Where did you get this, Patrick?"

"I ordered it from a comic book," said Patrick proudly.

"Then aliens must be real!" exclaimed SpongeBob. "Let's go spray the rocket ship!"

chapter three

SpongeBob and Patrick quietly walked up to Sandy's rocket ship. It was late at night. Sandy was fast asleep in her bed.

"Okay, Patrick," said SpongeBob, "we'll just spray the outside of the rocket ship so it'll be safe from aliens, and then we'll go home."

Patrick ran up to the ship and saw a button marked PRESS THIS TO GET INSIDE ROCKET SHIP.

"Hey! We can get inside the rocket," said Patrick.

"No, we can't!" cried SpongeBob. "We're just spraying the outside and going home!"

"But all I have to do is push this," said Patrick as he pushed the button. The door opened—right on top of SpongeBob!

"Ouch!" cried SpongeBob.

"I did it! I opened it!" cried Patrick. "Let's go inside!"

Patrick ran inside and SpongeBob followed.

Inside there were flashing lights and levers and video screens and buttons everywhere.

"Holy sea cow!" cried Patrick. "This must be the control room!"

"Don't touch anything!" warned SpongeBob.

It was too late. Patrick was sitting in a chair in front of a video monitor. He was pushing buttons and pulling levers. He thought it was a video game.

"Look! I'm winning!" yelled Patrick.

"Cut it out!" said SpongeBob. "We can't hang around in here. This is Sandy's rocket. Stop playing!"

"I won *again!*" cried Patrick.

"Really?" asked SpongeBob, peering over Patrick's shoulder. "Can I have a turn? Gee, what game is that?"

Patrick shrugged. "I don't know. But let's see what these other things do!"

And then he reached up and pulled more levers and pushed more buttons.

"I like rockets!" said Patrick.

"Stop touching buttons!" yelled SpongeBob.

Just then Patrick saw a very interesting button.

"Not even *this* button?" asked Patrick. "I bet this is the one that starts the rocket."

SpongeBob shook his head. "Patrick, pardon me for pulling rank, but *I'm* the space traveler here. And I happen to know that the button to start the spaceship is right over here!"

SpongeBob pointed to a red button.

"That's not it!" said Patrick.

"Yes it is!" said SpongeBob.

"Prove it!" said Patrick.

"Okay!" said SpongeBob, and he pressed the button.

The rocket began to roar and shake and make a lot of noise.

"Uh-oh," said SpongeBob.

Patrick pointed at SpongeBob and laughed. "*You* started the rocket! *You* started the rocket! Ha! Ha! Ha!"

All the noise woke Sandy up. She saw her rocket ship blasting off—to the moon!

She sat up in bed and yelled, "SPONGEBOB!"

chapter four

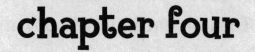

SpongeBob and Patrick were holding onto one another as the rocket ship shook, rattled, and rolled.

"Hold on, buddy!" yelled Patrick.

"I'm holding!" yelled SpongeBob.

The rocket shot out of the ocean and into the air.

"Good-bye, Bikini Bottom!" called SpongeBob.

The rocket went higher and higher into the sky.

Suddenly SpongeBob and Patrick began to float in the air.

"Help! Somebody get me down!" cried Patrick as he floated toward the top of the rocket. Then he turned upside down. "Help! Somebody get me up!"

SpongeBob looked out the window and saw the black sky filled with stars. Millions of stars. "We're in outer space!" he yelled.

SpongeBob and Patrick started to have fun, turning somersaults and floating in the air.

"I'm a bird!" said Patrick.

"I'm a balloon!" cried SpongeBob.

The rocket ship was headed right for the moon. Exactly as Sandy had programmed it.

But SpongeBob and Patrick weren't paying attention to where the rocket ship was going. They were too busy flying and floating.

Patrick kept banging into the walls and

hitting buttons. He hit so many buttons, he changed the direction of the rocket ship. The rocket ship went right around the moon and headed back toward Earth!

SpongeBob and Patrick didn't notice. They were having too much fun.

Meanwhile, back in Bikini Bottom, Sandy was strapping on a rocket jet pack. It allowed her to lift off into space all by herself.

As she tightened the straps, she shook her head. "Sometimes that SpongeBob is as dumb as a sack of peanuts! What the heck did he think he was doing, taking off in my rocket? I better get up there on the moon before he gets into more trouble!"

Sandy blasted off in her rocket jet pack, never seeing the rocket carrying SpongeBob and Patrick as it splashed back into the water.

chapter five

As the rocket ship came out of space, SpongeBob and Patrick stopped floating and fell to the floor.

"I'm not a bird anymore!" said Patrick.

"We must be landing on the moon!" exclaimed SpongeBob.

"All right!" yelled Patrick.

SpongeBob and Patrick put on their space suits and filled them with water so they wouldn't dry out.

"Patrick, prepare to walk on the moon!" proclaimed SpongeBob.

"Aye, aye, Captain!" replied Patrick.

SpongeBob carefully opened the door of the rocket ship. They popped their heads out and saw . . . Squidward's tiki house and SpongeBob's pineapple house and Patrick's rock.

"Wow . . . the moon sure looks a lot like home," said Patrick.

"Good!" said SpongeBob. "We won't feel homesick."

SpongeBob carefully stepped out onto the sand. "This is one small step for a sponge, one giant leap for spongekind!"

Just then Gary, SpongeBob's pet snail, came crawling by.

Patrick pointed. "Hey, look! It's Gary!"

"Meow," said Gary.

"Come here, Gary!" cried Patrick as he started to run toward him.

SpongeBob grabbed Patrick. "Stop! Don't go near him!"

"Why not?" asked Patrick.

"This is all a trick!" warned SpongeBob. "The aliens are projecting our memories onto the environment! They want us to think this is Bikini Bottom, but it's *really* the moon. They're trying to confuse us!"

Patrick scratched his head. "You mean to say they've taken what we thought we think and made us think we thought our thoughts we've been thinking are thoughts we think we thought?"

SpongeBob nodded. "I couldn't have said it better! But we're not going to fall for it!"

SpongeBob aimed the moon rock harvester popgun at Gary. "You who are not Gary, but pretend to be Gary, prepare to be harvested!"

SpongeBob pushed the button on the moon rock harvester. *ZAP!*

Suddenly Gary was wrapped up in a net.

SpongeBob grinned. "Now what do you have to say for yourself, Mr. Alien?"

"Meow," said Gary.

"You got 'em, SpongeBob! What a shot!" cried Patrick. "Boy, is Sandy gonna be proud!"

SpongeBob turned pale. "Sandy! Oh, no! I forgot all about her! She's going to be really mad at us for stealing her rocket!"

SpongeBob didn't know what to do. He couldn't stand the idea of Sandy being mad at him. He was trying to think of something he could say or do when Gary meowed again.

"That's it!" said SpongeBob. "Sandy won't hate us when I bring her back a real live alien! Or two! Or three! Or four! Or more! She'll love me! Come, Patrick! Let the alien harvesting begin!"

chapter six

SpongeBob raced across the sand toward Squidward's house.

Patrick followed and began to yell excitedly, "Oh, boy! Alien hunting! Alien hunting!"

"Quiet, Patrick!" whispered SpongeBob. "We can't let the aliens know we're on to them."

SpongeBob then spoke loudly so anyone nearby could hear. "Oh, yeah! *Alien Hunting*. That was a great TV show! Amazing special effects!"

SpongeBob motioned for Patrick to follow him to Squidward's front door. "Hey, Patrick!" he shouted. "Let's go visit our good old friend Squidward and see what he's up to!"

SpongeBob knocked on the door.

No one answered.

They quietly pushed the door open and went inside.

"Make sure your alien harvester popgun is ready to go," whispered SpongeBob as they walked into Squidward's bedroom.

Squidward was asleep in his bed. His four little bunny slippers were next to his bed on the floor.

"That is one ugly alien," said SpongeBob.

"It's disgusting!" added Patrick.

Squidward was dreaming and talking in his sleep, "Uh . . . no . . . Grandma . . . don't take away my clarinet . . . I'll be a good squid."

SpongeBob and Patrick walked right up to Squidward's bed and looked down at him as he slept.

"It's even uglier up close," whispered SpongeBob. "Let's begin the alien examination."

SpongeBob pulled back Squidward's blanket. Squidward was wearing a nightshirt with little bears and ducks on it.

Patrick looked closer. "Look! There's something underneath the alien!"

SpongeBob saw something red and rubbery under Squidward's body.

"I think I'm going to be sick!" said Patrick.

SpongeBob pulled it out. It was only Squidward's rubber hot-water bottle. He used it at night to keep himself warm.

But SpongeBob thought it was something else. He held it up to Patrick. "Do you know what this is?" he asked.

"It's stinky!" replied Patrick.

"No," said SpongeBob. "It's an egg sack!"

"It's a stinky egg sack," said Patrick.

SpongeBob continued. "This disgusting alien creature has laid an egg, and if I'm correct, it is filled with baby aliens!"

"Now I *know* I'm gonna be sick!" cried Patrick.

SpongeBob held the hot-water bottle up to the lamp next to Squidward's bed. The light shone behind the hot-water bottle and showed the silhouette of SpongeBob's two hands.

"Twins!" cried SpongeBob. "Horrible, disgusting, evil alien twins!"

Just then Squidward turned over and one of his tentacles landed on Patrick's face.

SPLAT!

"Help! Get this thing off of me!" screamed Patrick.

SpongeBob quickly reached up to pull Squidward's tentacle off of Patrick's face.

It was stuck!

"Don't let the alien get me, SpongeBob!" cried Patrick.

"I won't!" yelled SpongeBob.

With all the noise and yelling, Squidward woke up. "Patrick! SpongeBob! What are you doing in my bedroom? Give me back my tentacle!" Squidward pulled his tentacle off Patrick's face.

"The evil, disgusting thing is awake!" cried SpongeBob.

"Hey! Watch who you're calling evil and disgusting!" yelled Squidward.

"Let's capture the little phony!" said SpongeBob.

"Get away from me!" yelled Squidward as he jumped out of his bed.

Squidward tried to run away, but Patrick tackled him.

"Ouch!" cried Squidward.

"Hold him, Patrick!" yelled SpongeBob as he got his moon rock harvester ready and aimed it at Squidward.

"SpongeBob!" cried a terrified Squidward. "What in the name of Neptune are you doing?"

"What any other patriotic Bikini Bottom citizen would do!" declared SpongeBob.

ZAP!

chapter seven

Mr. Krabs, SpongeBob's boss, and owner of the Krusty Krab, was out taking his sea snake for a late-night walk.

Mr. Krabs was thinking of all the money he had made that day. Suddenly he heard a strange noise and saw SpongeBob and Patrick coming out of Squidward's house. They were carrying a very mysterious-looking bag.

"Ahoy there, lads! Up a bit late to be playing pirate, aren't ya? Got yourselves a new mate?"

asked Mr. Krabs with a laugh.

SpongeBob nudged Patrick. "It's another alien! Let's get him!"

They both pulled out their popguns and aimed them at Mr. Krabs.

Mr. Krabs was terrified. "No! Don't shoot me!"

SpongeBob got him in his sights. "Ready, aim—"

Mr. Krabs held up his pincers. "Wait a minute! On second thought, go ahead and shoot me! Just don't take me sweet, lovely money!"

"We don't want your money, moon man!" said SpongeBob.

Mr. Krabs breathed a sigh of relief. "Well, that be the best news I've heard all day!"

"We want you!" shouted Patrick.

ZAP!

And the next thing he knew, Mr. Krabs was caught in a net.

"SpongeBob!" yelled Mr. Krabs. "If you don't let me out of here, you'll never flip another Krabby Patty as long as you live!"

"Nice try, alien!" said SpongeBob.

Meanwhile Sandy had landed on the moon. She looked and looked and looked, but there was no SpongeBob and no rocket ship.

"Where did that knucklehead go?" she wondered. "He must've gone back to Bikini Bottom. I'd better get back there too."

She pushed the button on her rocket jet pack and blasted off for home.

Down in Bikini Bottom, SpongeBob and Patrick went back to the rocket ship. They tossed the nets with Squidward and Mr. Krabs into the cargo hold with Gary.

"Ouch!" cried Squidward.

"Ow!" yelled Mr. Krabs.

"Meow," said Gary.

SpongeBob stared at the three of them. "Look at them! Squirming around in there like a bunch of ugly, disgusting aliens!"

"They're gross!" said Patrick.

SpongeBob closed the hatch. "It's a tough job, but someone has to do it! And that someone is us! We have a mission, Patrick. It's time for an alien roundup!"

SpongeBob and Patrick went to Mrs. Puff's Boating School.

Mrs. Puff was correcting papers at her desk when she looked up and saw them coming into her room.

"SpongeBob SquarePants! Patrick Star!" said Mrs. Puff. "What are you doing here so late?"

SpongeBob sneered. "We'll ask the questions here, Mrs. Puff! If that *is* your real name, and I happen to know it *isn't!*"

Mrs. Puff angrily stood up. "SpongeBob! You are going to sit in the corner and think about what you just said!"

"School's out, sister!" yelled SpongeBob.

Mrs. Puff started to scream but it was too late. *ZAP!*

As they dragged her out of the schoolroom in her net, Mrs. Puff yelled, "This is going on your permanent record, SpongeBob!"

SpongeBob and Patrick continued to round up everyone in Bikini Bottom.

They found Pearl, Mr. Krabs's daughter, at the Whale Watchers Mall. She was so big, being a whale, that they had to use six nets to capture her!

"Excuse me!" she complained. "But this net does *not* go with my outfit!"

Next they captured Plankton, the owner of Plankton's Chum Bucket and the smallest resident of Bikini Bottom. He was trying to sneak into the Krusty Krab to steal a Krabby Patty.

"At last I will have the secret recipe for Krabby Patties and the world will be mine!" Plankton bellowed.

"Not so fast!" cried SpongeBob.

"You're an alien and you're going down!" said Patrick.

"Ha! You'll never get me!" yelled Plankton.

ZAP!

"You got me," said Plankton sadly.

chapter eight

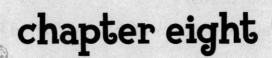

Soon the entire population of Bikini Bottom was wrapped up in nets. SpongeBob and Patrick were pushing them into the cargo hold of the rocket ship. It was getting very crowded.

"SpongeBob, we've got a problem," said Patrick. "They can't all fit in the rocket ship!"

"Just push harder!" said SpongeBob. "We must get all of the aliens!"

"We're not *aliens!*" screamed Squidward from inside his net.

"Hah! That's what they *all* say," said SpongeBob.

"Of course we're *all* saying it! It's true!" roared Mr. Krabs.

"I have to get back to the mall!" cried Pearl.

"I have test papers to correct!" said Mrs. Puff.

"Give me liberty or give me the recipe to Krabby Patties!" screamed Plankton.

"Don't listen to them, Patrick," warned SpongeBob. "They're just trying to confuse us with their evil alien ways!"

They were pushing the last "alien" into the rocket ship when suddenly they heard a noise coming from above.

"Look, SpongeBob!" cried Patrick. "It's Sandy!"

Sandy was floating down toward them. "SpongeBob! What are y'all doing? I can't turn my back on you for two whole seconds without

you causin' a heap of trouble!"

"Help us, Sandy!" yelled Squidward.

Sandy landed on the ocean floor and looked into the cargo hold. She saw everyone from Bikini Bottom wrapped up in nets.

"What the heck is going on here?" asked Sandy. "Bagging up all your friends and neighbors just like they were a fresh crop of hickory-smoked sausages! You done turned my little science experiment into a disaster! You ought to be ashamed of yourselves!"

SpongeBob aimed his alien harvester popgun at Sandy.

"Nice try, Ms. Alien, but I'm not falling for it!" said SpongeBob.

"Are you sure that's not the real Sandy?" asked Patrick.

"Zap now. Ask questions later," said SpongeBob.

Sandy glared at SpongeBob. "Why are you aiming that moon rock harvester at me?"

"Because *you* are an alien," said SpongeBob. "And it's not a moon rock harvester, it's an alien harvester!"

ZAP!

And then Sandy was in a net, just like the others. SpongeBob and Patrick tossed her into the cargo hold.

"Aliens!" exclaimed Sandy. "Is that what this is all about? You think we're all aliens?"

SpongeBob pushed the button to close the cargo door hatch.

The door slowly closed as Sandy kept yelling, "This isn't the moon! You're still in Bikini—"

The door closed. Neither SpongeBob nor Patrick heard her.

SpongeBob shook his head. "Just goes to show you, Patrick, you can't trust anyone!

Anybody could be an alien! Even . . ."

SpongeBob looked at Patrick suspiciously.

"Patrick! You were an alien all along!" said SpongeBob.

"I was?" asked Patrick.

"And you didn't even tell me!" said SpongeBob.

SpongeBob aimed his zapper at Patrick. Patrick aimed his zapper at SpongeBob. "Not so fast! It's not you that's got me . . . it's . . . it's me that's got me!"

And with that, Patrick turned his popgun around and zapped himself right in the face, wrapping himself in a net.

"Help! I'm an alien!" cried Patrick.

chapter nine

SpongeBob threw Patrick in the cargo hold. Then he got in the rocket ship and raced up to the control room.

SpongeBob smiled as he pushed the BLAST OFF button. "Boy, I can't wait to see the look on Sandy's face when I get back to Bikini Bottom with all these aliens! She's gonna think I'm the greatest guy in the world!"

SpongeBob set the controls for extra super fast.

The rocket ship zoomed through space, carrying its cargo of confused sea creatures.

"Bikini Bottom here we come!" he yelled.

When the rocket ship landed, SpongeBob ran out and yelled, "Hey, Sandy! I'm back! Come see what I found!"

He stopped.

He looked around.

He didn't see his pineapple house or Squidward's tiki house or Patrick's rock or even the Krusty Krab.

All he saw were craters and rocks and more craters and rocks.

Wow, he thought to himself, Bikini Bottom sure has changed.

And then SpongeBob looked up in the sky and saw . . . the Earth.

"Uh-oh," said SpongeBob.

"SPONGEBOB!" yelled Sandy, Squidward,

Patrick, Mr. Krabs, Mrs. Puff, Pearl, and all the other Bikini Bottom residents.

SpongeBob opened the cargo hold.

"Uh . . . there seems to have been a little mistake," said SpongeBob.

"Get us out of here!" shouted Sandy.

SpongeBob let everybody out of the nets.

"What do you have to say for yourself, SpongeBob?" asked Squidward.

"I'm sorry," cried SpongeBob. "It was all my fault! I was blinded by science! You all go back home. I'll stay on the moon. That will be my punishment! Banished from Bikini Bottom forever!"

"Sounds good to me!" said Squidward.

"Aw heck, we can't leave SpongeBob here," said Sandy. "Bikini Bottom wouldn't be the same without him."

"I agree!" said SpongeBob.

And so they all blasted off for home.

Sandy steered the rocket ship back toward Earth.

"SpongeBob, I hope you learned your lesson," said Sandy.

"Oh, I have," said SpongeBob. "Never go into your friend's rocket ship without her permission. Never fly to the moon. And *never* catch all your friends in nets because you think they are aliens."

"That's pretty close, I reckon," she said.

"So, Sandy?" asked SpongeBob. "Where are we going next? Mars? Venus? Pluto? . . ."

"Settle down, SpongeBob. I can't concentrate!"

". . . Jupiter, Saturn, Uranus?" SpongeBob continued.

"I know *exactly where you're* going," said Sandy.

"Where?" asked SpongeBob excitedly. "Will I get to catch aliens?"

ZAP!

And with that, Sandy shot her popgun at SpongeBob, wrapped him in a net, and put him in the cargo hold.

"Oh, no!" screamed Patrick. "SpongeBob is an alien!"

Sandy shook her head.

It was going to be a long trip back to Bikini Bottom.